"Nobody knows me better than you do, Poppy.

I have faith that you'll pick the right wife for me."

With those awful words still ringing in the room, Isaiah left her there, sitting at her desk, feeling numb.

The fact of the matter was, she probably *could* pick him a perfect wife. Someone who would facilitate his life and give him space when he needed it. Someone who was beautiful and fabulous in bed.

Yes, she knew exactly what Isaiah Grayson would think made a woman the perfect wife for him.

And what she so desperately wanted was for Isaiah's perfect wife to be *her*.

But dreams were for other women. In her experience, they always had been.

Which meant some other woman was going to end up with Poppy's dream.

While she played matchmaker to the whole affair.

\* \* \*

*Want Me, Cowboy* is part of the
Copper Ridge series from *New York Times*
bestselling author Maisey Yates!

# MAISEY YATES

——

## WANT ME, COWBOY

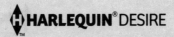

**HARLEQUIN**® DESIRE

Recycling programs
for this product may
not exist in your area.

ISBN-13: 978-1-335-97183-8

Want Me, Cowboy

Copyright © 2018 by Maisey Yates

This edition published by arrangement with Harlequin Books S.A.

For questions and comments about the quality of this book, please contact us at CustomerService@Harlequin.com.

Printed in U.S.A.

In Copper Ridge, Oregon, lasting love with a
cowboy is only a happily-ever-after away.
Don't miss any of Maisey Yates's
Copper Ridge tales, available now!

## From Harlequin Desire

*Take Me, Cowboy*
*Hold Me, Cowboy*
*Seduce Me, Cowboy*
*Claim Me, Cowboy*
*Want Me, Cowboy*

## From HQN Books

*Shoulda Been a Cowboy* (prequel novella)
*Part Time Cowboy*
*Brokedown Cowboy*
*Bad News Cowboy*
*A Copper Ridge Christmas* (ebook novella)
*The Cowboy Way*
*Hometown Heartbreaker* (ebook novella)
*One Night Charmer*
*Tough Luck Hero*
*Last Chance Rebel*
*Slow Burn Cowboy*
*Down Home Cowboy*
*Wild Ride Cowboy*
*Christmastime Cowboy*

For more books by Maisey Yates,
visit www.maiseyyates.com.

# One

November 1, 2018
Location: Copper Ridge, Oregon

WIFE WANTED—

Rich rancher, not given to socializing. Wants a wife who will not try to change me. Must be tolerant of moods, reported lack of sensitivity and the tendency to take off for a few days' time in the mountains. Will expect meals cooked. Also, probably a kid or two. Exact number to be negotiated. Beard is nonnegotiable.

November 5, 2018
Revised draft for approval by 11/6

### WIFE WANTED—

~~Rich rancher, not given to socializing.~~ Successful rancher searching for a wife who enjoys rural living. ~~Wants a wife who will not try to change me. Must be tolerant of moods, reported lack of sensitivity, and the tendency to take off for a few days' time in the mountains.~~ Though happy with my life, it has begun to feel lonely, and I would like someone to enhance my satisfaction with what I have already. I enjoy extended camping trips and prefer the mountains to a night on the town. ~~Will expect meals cooked. Also, probably a kid or two. Exact number to be negotiated. Beard is non-negotiable. I~~ I'm looking for a traditional family life, and a wife and children to share it with.

"This is awful."

Poppy Sinclair looked up from her desk, her eyes colliding with her boss's angry gray stare. He was holding a printout of the personal ad she'd revised for him and shaking it at her like she was a dog and it was a newspaper.

"The *original* was awful," she responded curtly, turning her focus back to her computer.

"But it was all true."

"Lead with being less of an asshole."

"I *am* an asshole," Isaiah said, clearly unconcerned with that fact.

He was at peace with himself. Which she admired on some level. Isaiah was Isaiah, and he made no apologies for that fact. But his attitude would be a problem if the man wanted to find a wife. Because very few other people were at peace with him just as he was.

"I would never say I want to—" he frowned "'—enhance my enjoyment.' What the hell, Poppy?"

Poppy had known Isaiah since she was eighteen years old. She was used to his moods. His complete lack of subtlety. His gruffness.

But somehow, she'd never managed to get used to *him*. As a man.

This grumpy, rough, bearded man who was like a brick wall. Or like one of those mountains he'd disappear into for days at a time.

Every time she saw him, it felt as if he'd stolen the air right from her lungs. It was more than just being handsome—though he was. A lot of men were handsome. His brother Joshua was handsome, and a whole lot easier to get along with.

Isaiah was… Well, he was her very particular brand of catnip. He made everything in her sit up, purr…and want to be stroked.

Even when he was in full hermit mode.

People—and interacting with them—were decidedly not his thing. It was one reason Poppy had always been an asset to him in his work life. It was her job to sit and take notes during meetings…and report her read on the room to him after. He was a brilliant businessman, and fantastic with numbers. But people…not so much.

As evidenced by the ad. Of course, the very fact that he was placing an ad to find a wife was both contradicting to that point—suddenly, he wanted a wife!—and also, somehow, firmly in affirmation of it. He was placing an ad to find her.

The whole situation was Joshua's fault. Well, probably Devlin and Joshua combined, in fairness.

Isaiah's brothers had been happy bachelors until a couple of years ago when Devlin had married their sister Faith's best friend, Mia.

Then, Joshua had been the next to succumb to matrimony, a victim of their father's harebrained scheme. The patriarch of the Grayson family had put an ad in a national newspaper looking for a wife for his son. In retaliation, Joshua had placed an ad of his own, looking for an unsuitable wife that would teach his father not to meddle.

It all backfired. Or…front fired. Either way, Joshua had ended up married to Danielle, and was now happily settled with her and her infant half brother who both of them were raising as their son.

It was after their wedding that Isaiah had formed his plan.

The wedding had—he had explained to Poppy at work one morning—clarified a few things for him.

He believed in marriage as a valuable institution, one that he wanted to be part of. He wanted stability. He wanted children. But he didn't have any inclination toward love.

He didn't have to tell her why.

She *knew* why.

Rosalind.

But she wouldn't speak her foster sister's name out loud, and neither would he. But she remembered. The awful, awful fallout of Rosalind's betrayal.

His pain. Poppy's own conflicted feelings.

It was easy to remember her conflicted feelings, since she still had them.

He was staring at her now, those slate eyes hard and glinting with an energy she couldn't quite pin down. And with coldness, a coldness that hadn't been there before Rosalind. A coldness that told her and any other woman—loud and clear—that his heart was unavailable.

That didn't mean her own heart didn't twist every time he walked into the room. Every time he leaned closer to her—like he was doing now—and she got a hint of the scent of him. Rugged and pine-laden and basically lumberjack porn for her senses.

He was a contradiction, from his cowboy hat down to his boots. A numbers guy who loved the outdoors and was built like he belonged outside doing hard labor.

Dear God, he was problematic.

He made her dizzy. Those broad shoulders, shoulders she wanted to grab on to. Lean waist and hips—hips she wanted to wrap her legs around. And his forearms...all hard muscle. She wanted to lick them.

He turned her into a being made of sensual frustration, and no one else did that. Ever. Sadly, she seemed to have no effect on him at all.

"I'm not trying to mislead anyone," he said.

"Right. But you *are* trying to entice someone." The very thought made her stomach twist into a knot. But jealousy was pointless. If Isaiah wanted her... well, he would have wanted her by now.

He straightened, moving away from her and walking across the office. She nearly sagged with relief. "My money should do that." As if that solved every potential issue.

She bit back a weary sigh. "Would you like someone who was maybe...interested in who you are as a person?"

She knew that was a stupid question to ask of Isaiah Grayson. But she was his friend, as well as his employee. So it was kind of...her duty to work through this with him. Even if she didn't want him to do this at all.

And she didn't want him to find anyone.

Wow. Some friend she was.

But then, having...complex feelings for one's friend made emotional altruism tricky.

"As you pointed out," he said, his tone dry, "I'm an asshole."

"You were actually the one who said that. I said you *sounded* like one."

He waved his hand. "Either way, I'm not going to win Miss Congeniality in the pageant, and we both know that. Fine with me if somebody wants to get hitched and spend my money."

She sighed heavily, ignoring the fact that her heart felt an awful lot like paper that had been crumpled up into a tight, mutilated ball. "Why do you even *want* a wife, Isaiah?"

"I explained that to you already. Joshua is settled. Devlin is settled."

"Yes, they are. So why now?"

"I always imagined I would get married," he said simply. "I never intended to spend my whole life single."

"Is your biological clock ticking?" she asked drily.

"In a way," he said. "Again, it all comes back to logic. I'm close to my family, to my brothers. They'll have children sooner rather than later. Joshua and Danielle already have a son. Cousins should be close in age. It just makes sense."

She bit the inside of her cheek. "So you...just think you can decide it's time and then make it happen?"

"Yes. And I think Joshua's experience proves you can make anything work as long as you have a common goal. It *can* be like math."

She graduated from biting her cheek to her tongue. Isaiah was a numbers guy unto his soul. "Uh-huh."

She refused to offer even a pat agreement because she just thought he was wrong. Not that she knew much of anything about relationships of…any kind really.

She'd been shuffled around so many foster homes as a child, and it wasn't until she was in high school that she'd had a couple years of stability with one family. Which was where she'd met Rosalind, the one foster sibling Poppy was still in touch with. They'd shared a room and talked about a future where they were more than wards of the state.

In the years since, Poppy felt like she'd carved out a decent life for herself. But still, it wasn't like she'd ever had any romantic relationships to speak of.

Pining after your boss didn't count.

"The only aspect of going out and hooking up I like is the hooking up," he said.

She wanted to punch him for that unnecessary addition to the conversation. She sucked her cheek in and bit the inside of it too. "Great."

"When you think about it, making a relationship a transaction is smart. Marriage is a legal agreement. But you don't just get sex. You get the benefit of having your household kept, children…"

"Right. Children." She'd ignored his first mention of them, but… She pressed her hands to her stomach unconsciously. Then, she dropped them quickly.

She should not be thinking about Isaiah and children or the fact that he intended to have them with another woman.

*Confused feelings* was a cop-out. And it was hard to deny the truth when she was steeped in this kind of reaction to him, to his presence, to his plan, to his talk about children.

The fact of the matter was, she was tragically in love with him. And he'd never once seen her the way she saw him.

She'd met him through Rosalind. When Poppy had turned eighteen, she'd found herself released from her foster home with nowhere to go. Everything she owned was in an old canvas tote that a foster mom had given her years ago.

Rosalind had been the only person Poppy could think to call. The foster sister she'd bonded with in her last few years in care. She'd always kept in touch with Rosalind, even when Rosalind had moved to Seattle and got work.

Even when she'd started dating a wonderful man she couldn't say enough good things about.

She was the only lifeline Poppy had, and she'd reached for her. And Rosalind had come through. She'd had Poppy come to Rosalind's apartment, and then she'd arranged for a job interview with her boyfriend, who needed an assistant for a construction firm he was with.

In one afternoon, Poppy had found a place to live, gotten a job and lost her heart.

Of course, she had lost it, immediately and—in the fullness of time it had become clear—irrevocably, to the one man who was off-limits.

Her boss. Her foster sister's boyfriend. Isaiah Grayson.

Though his status as her boss had lasted longer than his status as Rosalind's boyfriend. He'd become her fiancé. And then after, her ex.

Poppy had lived with a divided heart for so long. Even after Isaiah and Rosalind's split, Poppy was able to care for them both. Though she never, ever spoke to Rosalind in Isaiah's presence, or even mentioned her.

Rosalind didn't have the same embargo on mentions of Isaiah. But in fairness, Rosalind was the one who had cheated on him, cost him a major business deal and nearly ruined his start-up company and—by extension—nearly ruined his relationship with his business partner, who was also his brother.

So.

Poppy had loved him while he'd dated another woman. Loved him while he nursed a broken heart because of said other woman. Loved him when he disavowed love completely. And now she would have to love him while she interviewed potential candidates to be his wife.

She was wretched.

He had said the word *sex* in front of her like it wouldn't do anything to her body. Had talked about children like it wouldn't make her…yearn.

Men were idiots. But this one might well be their king.

"Put the unrevised ad in the paper."

She shook her head. "I'm not doing that."

"I could fire you." He leaned in closer and her breath caught. "For insubordination."

Her heart tumbled around erratically, and she wished she could blame it on anger. Annoyance. But she knew that wasn't it.

She forced herself to rally. "If you haven't fired me yet, you're never going to. And anyway," she said, narrowing her tone so that the words would hit him with a point, "I'm the one who has to interview your prospective brides. Which makes this my endeavor in many ways. I'm the one who's going to have to weed through your choices. So I would like the ad to go out that I think has the best chance of giving me less crap to sort through."

He looked up at her, and much to her surprise seemed to be considering what she said. "That is true. You will be doing the interviews."

She felt like she'd been stabbed. She was going to be interviewing Isaiah's potential wife. The man she had been in love with since she was a teenage idiot, and was still in love with now that she was an idiot in her late twenties.

There were a whole host of reasons she'd never, ever let on about her feelings for him, Rosalind and his feelings on love aside.

She loved her job. She loved Isaiah's family, who she'd gotten to know well over the past decade, and who were the closest thing she had to a family of her own.

Plus, loving him was just…easy to dismiss. She wasn't the type of girl who could have something like that. Not Poppy Sinclair whose mother had disappeared when she was two years old and left her with a father who forgot to feed her.

Her life was changing though, slowly.

She was living well beyond what she had ever imagined would be possible for her. Gray Bear Construction was thriving; the merger between Jonathan Bear and the Graysons' company a couple of years ago was more successful than they'd imagined it could be.

And every employee on every level had reaped the benefits.

She was also living in the small town of Copper Ridge, Oregon, which was a bit strange for a girl from Seattle, but she did like it. It had a different pace. But that meant there was less opportunity for a social life. There were fewer people to interact with. By default she, and the other folks in town, ended up spending a lot of their free time with the people they worked with every day. There was nothing wrong with that. She loved Faith, and she had begun getting close to Joshua's wife recently. But it was just… Mostly there wasn't enough of a break from Isaiah on any given day.

But then, she also didn't enforce one. Didn't take one. She supposed she couldn't really blame the small-town location when the likely culprit of the entire situation was *her*.

"Place whatever ad you need to," he said, his tone abrupt. "When you meet the right woman, you'll know."

"I'll know," she echoed lamely.

"Yes. Nobody knows me better than you do, Poppy. I have faith that you'll pick the right wife for me."

With those awful words still ringing in the room, Isaiah left her there, sitting at her desk, feeling numb and ill used.

The fact of the matter was, she probably *could* pick him a perfect wife. Someone who would facilitate his life, and give him space when he needed it. Someone who was beautiful and fabulous in bed.

Yes, she knew exactly what Isaiah Grayson would think made a woman the perfect wife for him.

The sad thing was, Poppy didn't possess very many of those qualities herself.

And what she so desperately wanted was for Isaiah's perfect wife to be *her*.

But dreams were for other women. They always had been. Which meant some other woman was going to end up with Poppy's dream.

While she played matchmaker to the whole affair.

# Two

"I put an ad in the paper."

"For?" Isaiah's brother Joshua looked up from his computer and stared at him like he was waiting to hear the answers to the mystery of the universe.

Joshua, Isaiah and their younger sister, Faith, were sitting in the waiting area of their office, enjoying their early-morning coffee. Or maybe enjoying was overstating it. The three of them were trying to find a state of consciousness.

"A wife."

Faith spat her coffee back into her cup. "What?"

"I placed an ad in the paper to help me find a wife," he repeated.

Honestly, he couldn't understand why she was

having such a large reaction to the news. After all, that was how Joshua had found his wife, Danielle.

"You can't be serious," Joshua said.

"I expected you of all people to be supportive."

"Why *me*?"

"Because that's how you met Danielle. Or you have you forgotten?"

"I have not forgotten how I met my wife. However, I didn't put an ad out there seriously thinking I was going to find someone to marry. I was trying to prove to dad that *his* ad was a stupid idea."

"But it turned out it wasn't a stupid idea," Isaiah said. "I want to get married. I figured this was a hassle-free way of finding a wife."

Faith stared at him, dumbfounded. "You can't be serious."

"I'm serious."

The door to the office opened, and Poppy walked in wearing a cheerful, polka-dotted dress, her dark hair swept back into a bun, a few curls around her face.

"Please tell me my brother is joking," Faith said. "And that he didn't actually put an ad in the paper to find a wife."

Poppy looked from him back to Faith. "He doesn't joke, you know that."

"And you know that he put an ad in the paper for a wife?" Joshua asked.

"Of course I know," Poppy responded. "Who do you think is doing the interviews?"

That earned him two slack-jawed looks.

"Who else is going to do it?" Isaiah asked.

"You're not even doing the interview for your own wife?" Faith asked.

"I trust Poppy implicitly. If I didn't, she wouldn't be my assistant."

"Of all the… You are insane." Faith stormed out of the room. Joshua continued to sit and sip his coffee.

"No comment?" Isaiah asked.

"Oh, I have plenty. But I know you well enough to know that making them won't change a damn thing. So I'm keeping my thoughts to myself. However," he said, collecting his computer and his coffee, "I do have to go to work now."

That left both Isaiah and Poppy standing in the room by themselves. She wasn't looking at him; she was staring off down the hall, her expression unreadable. She had a delicate profile, dark, sweeping eyelashes and a fascinating curve to her lips. Her neck was long and elegant, and the way her dress shaped around her full breasts was definitely a pleasing sight.

He clenched his teeth. He didn't make a habit of looking at Poppy that way. But she was pretty. He had always thought so.

Even back when he'd been with Rosalind he'd thought there was something…indefinable about Poppy. Special.

She made him feel… He didn't know. A little

more grounded. Or maybe it was just because she treated him differently than most people did.

Either way, she was irreplaceable to him. In the running of his business, Poppy was his barometer. The way he got the best read on a situation. She did his detail work flawlessly. Handled everything he didn't like so he could focus on what he was good at.

She was absolutely, 100 percent, the most important asset to him at the company.

He would have to tell her that sometime. Maybe buy her another pearl necklace. Though, last time he'd done that she had gotten angry at him. But she wore it. She was wearing it today, in fact.

"They're right," she said finally.

"About?"

"The fact that you're insane."

"I think I'm sane enough."

"Of course you do. Actually—" she let out a long, slow breath "—I don't think you're insane. But, I don't think this is a good idea."

"Why?"

"This is really how you want to find a wife? In a way that's this…impersonal?"

"What are my other options? I have to meet someone new, go through the process of dating… She'll expect a courtship of some kind. We'll have to figure out what we have in common, what we don't have in common. This way, it's all out in the open. That's more straightforward."

"Maybe you deserve better than that," she said, her tone uncharacteristically gentle.

"Maybe this is better for *me*."

She shook her head. "I don't know about that."

"When it comes to matters of business, there's no one I trust more than you. But you're going to have to trust that I know what will work best in my own life."

"It's not what I want for you."

A strange current arced between them when she spoke those words, a spark in her brown eyes catching on something inside him.

"I appreciate your concern."

"Yes," she echoed. "My concern."

"We have work to do. And you have wife applications to sort through."

"Right," she said.

"Preference will be given to blondes," he said.

Poppy blinked and then reached up slowly, touching her own dark hair. "Of course."

And then she turned and walked out of the room.

Isaiah hadn't expected to receive quite so many responses to his ad. Perhaps, in the end, Poppy had been right about her particular tactic with the wording. It had certainly netted what felt to him to be a record number of responses.

Though he didn't actually know how many women had responded to his brother's personal ad.

He felt only slightly competitive about it, seeing as it would be almost impossible to do a direct comparison between his and Joshua's efforts. Their father had placed an ad first, making Joshua sound undoubtedly even nicer than Poppy had made Isaiah sound.

Thereafter, Joshua had placed his own ad, which had offered a fake marriage and hefty compensation.

Isaiah imagined that a great many more women would respond to that.

But he didn't need quantity. He just needed quality.

And he believed that existed.

It had occurred to him at Joshua and Danielle's wedding that there was no reason a match couldn't be like math. He believed in marriage; it was romance he had gone off of.

Or rather, the kind of romance he had experience with.

Obviously, he couldn't dispute the existence of love. His parents were in love, after all. Forty years of marriage hadn't seemed to do anything to dampen that. But then, he was not like his mother. And he wasn't like his father. Both of them were warm people. *Compassionate.* And those things seemed to come easily to them.

Isaiah was a black-and-white man living in a world filled with shades of gray. He didn't care for those shades, and he didn't like to acknowledge them.

But he wasn't an irrational man. Not at all.

Yet he'd been irrational once. Five years with Rosalind and they had been the best of his life. At least, he had thought so at the time.

Then she had betrayed him, and nearly destroyed everything.

Or rather, he had.

Which was all he had needed to learn about what happened to him and his instincts under the influence of love.

He'd been in his twenties then, and it had been easy to ignore the idea that his particular set of practices when it came to relationships meant he would be spending his life without a partner. But now he was in his thirties, and that reality was much more difficult to ignore. When he'd had to think about the future, he hadn't liked the idea of what he was signing himself up for.

So, he had decided to change it. That was the logical thing to do when you found yourself unhappy with where you were, after all. A change of circumstances was not beyond his reach. And so, he was reaching out to grab it.

Which was why Poppy was currently on interview number three with one of the respondents to his ad. Isaiah had insisted that anyone responding to the ad come directly to Copper Ridge to be interviewed. Anyone who didn't take the ad seriously enough to put in a personal appearance was not worthy of consideration, in his opinion.

He leaned back in his chair, looking at the neat expanse of desk in front of him. Everything was in its place in his office, as it always was. As it should be. And soon, everything in his personal life would be in place too.

Across the hall, the door to Poppy's office opened and a tall, willowy blonde walked out. She was definitely his type in the physical sense, and the physical mattered quite a bit. Emotionally, he might be a bit detached, but physically, everything was functioning. Quite well, thank you.

In his marriage-math equation, sex was an important factor.

He intended to be faithful to his wife. There was really no point in making a lifelong commitment without fidelity.

Because of that, it stood to reason that he should make sure he chose in accordance with his typical physical type.

By the time he finished that thought process the woman was gone, and Poppy appeared a moment later. She was glaring down the hall, looking both disheveled and generally irritated. He had learned to recognize her moods with unerring accuracy. Mostly because it was often a matter of survival. Poppy was one of the few people on earth who wasn't intimidated by him. He should be annoyed by that. She was his employee, and ought to be a bit more deferential than she was.

He didn't want her to be, though. He liked Poppy. And that was a rarity in his world. He didn't like very many people. Because most people were idiots.

But not her.

Though, she looked a little bit like she wanted to kill him at the moment. When her stormy, dark eyes connected with his across the space, he had the fleeting thought that a lesser man would jump up and run away, leaving his boots behind.

Isaiah was not that man.

He was happy to meet her. Steel-capped toe to pointy-toed stiletto.

"She was stupid," Poppy pronounced.

He lifted a brow. "Did you give her an IQ test?"

"I'm not talking about her intelligence," Poppy said, looking fierce. "Though, the argument could be made that any woman responding to this ad…"

"Are you about to cast aspersions on my desirability?"

"No," she said. "I cast those last week, if you recall. It would just be tiresome to cast them again."

"Why is she stupid?" he pressed.

"Because she has no real concept of what you need. You're a busy man, and you live in a rural… area. You're not going to be taking her out to galas every night. And I know she thought that because you're a rich man galas were going to be part of the deal. But I explained to her that you only go to a certain number of business-oriented events a year, and that you do so grudgingly. That anyone hanging on your arm at such a thing would need to be polished, smiling, and, in general, making up for you."

He spent a moment deciding if he should be offended by that or not. He decided not to be. Because she was right. He knew his strengths and his limitations.

"She didn't seem very happy about those details. And that is why I'm saying she's stupid. She wants to take this...job, essentially. A job that is a life sentence. And she wants it to be about her."

He frowned. "Obviously, this marriage is not going to be completely about me. I am talking about a *marriage* and not a position at the company." Though, he supposed he could see why she would be thinking in those terms. He had placed an ad with strict requirements. And he supposed, as a starting point, it *was* about him.

"Is that true, Isaiah? Because I kind of doubt it. You don't want a woman who's going to inconvenience you."

"I'm not buying a car," he said.

"Aren't you?" She narrowed her eyes, her expression mean.

"No. I realize that."

"You're basically making an arranged marriage for yourself."

"Consider it advanced online dating," he said. "With a more direct goal."

"You're having your assistant choose a wife for you." She enunciated each word as if he didn't understand what he'd asked of her.

Her delicate brows locked together, and her mouth pulled into a pout. Though, she would undoubtedly punch him if he called it a pout.

In a physical sense, Poppy was not his type at all. She was not tall, or particularly leggy, though she did often wear high heels with her 1950s housewife dresses. She was petite, but still curvy, her hair dark and curly, and usually pulled back in a loose, artfully pinned bun that allowed tendrils to slowly make their escape over the course of the day.

She was pretty, in spite of the fact that she wasn't the type of woman he would normally gravitate toward.

He wasn't sure why he was just now noticing that. Perhaps it was the way the light was filtering through the window now. Falling across her delicately curved face. Her mahogany skin with a bit of rose color bleeding across her cheeks. In this instance, he had a feeling the color was because she was angry. But, it was lovely nonetheless.

Her lips were full—pouty or not—and the same rose color as her cheeks.

"I don't understand your point," he said, stopping his visual perusal of her.

"I'm just saying you're taking about as much of a personal interest in finding a wife as someone who was buying a car."

He did not point out that if he were buying a car, he would take it for a test drive, and that he had not suggested doing anything half so crass with any of the women who'd come to be interviewed.

"How many more women are you seeing today?"

he asked, deciding to bypass her little show of indignation.

"Three more," she said.

There was something in the set of her jaw, in the rather stubborn, mulish look on her face that almost made him want to ask a question about what was bothering her.

But only almost.

"Has my sister sent through cost estimates for her latest design?" he asked.

Poppy blinked. "What?"

"Faith. Has she sent through her cost estimates? I'm going to end up correcting them anyway, but I like to see what she starts with."

"I'm well aware of the process, Isaiah," Poppy said. "I'm just surprised that you moved on from wife interviews to your sister's next design."

"Why would you be surprised by that? The designs are important. They are, in fact, why I am a billionaire."

"Yes. I know," Poppy said. "Faith's talent is a big reason why we're all doing well. Believe me, I respect the work. However, the subject change seems a bit abrupt."

"It *is* a workday."

Deep brown eyes narrowed in his direction. "You're really something else, do you know that?"

He did. He always had. The fact that she felt the need to question him on it didn't make much sense to him.

"Yes," he responded.

Poppy stamped.

She stamped her high-heel-clad foot like they were in a black-and-white movie.

"No, she hasn't sent it through," Poppy said.

"You just stomped your foot at me."

She flung her arms wide. "Because you were just being an idiot at me."

"I don't understand you," he said.

"I don't need you to understand me." Her brow furrowed.

"But you *do* need me to sign your paychecks," he pointed out. "I'm your boss."

Then, all the color drained from her cheeks. "Right. Of course. I do need that. Because you're my boss."

"I am."

"Just my boss."

"I've been your boss for the past decade," he pointed out, not quite sure why she was being so spiky.

"Yes," she said. "You have been my boss for the past decade."

Then, she turned on her heel and walked back into her office, shutting the door firmly behind her.

And Isaiah went back to his desk.

He had work to do. Which was why he had given Poppy the task of picking him a wife. But before he chased Faith down for those estimates, he was going to need some caffeine. He sent a quick text to that effect to Poppy.

There was a quick flash of three dots at the bottom of the message box, then they disappeared.

It popped up again, and disappeared again. Then finally there was a simple: of course.

He could only hope that when he got his coffee it wasn't poisoned.

Three hours and three women later, Poppy was wishing she had gone with her original instinct and sent the middle finger emoji to Isaiah in response to his request for coffee.

This was too much. It would be crazy for anyone to have their assistant pick their wife—a harebrained scheme that no self-respecting personal assistant should have to cope with. But for her especially, it was a strange kind of emotional torture. She had to ask each woman questions about their compatibility with Isaiah. And then, she had to talk to them about Isaiah. Who she knew better than she knew any other man on the face of the earth. Who she knew possibly better than she knew anyone else. And all the while his words rang in her ears.

*I'm your boss.*

She was his *employee*.

And that was how he saw her. It shouldn't surprise her that no-nonsense, rigid Isaiah thought of her primarily as his employee. She thought of him as her friend.

Her best friend. Practically family.

Except for the part of her that was in love with him and had sex dreams about him sometimes.

Though, were she to take an afternoon nap today, her only dreams about Isaiah would involve her sticking a pen through his chest.

Well, maybe not his chest. That would be fatal. Maybe his arm. But then, that would get ink and blood on his shirt. She would have to unbutton it and take it off him…

Okay. Maybe she was capable of having both dreams at the same time.

"Kittens are my hard line," the sixth blonde of the day was saying to her. All the blondes were starting to run together like boxes of dye in the hair care aisle.

"I…" Poppy blinked, trying to get a handle on what that meant. "Like… Sexually… Or?"

The woman wrinkled her nose. "I mean, I need to be able to have a kitten. That's nonnegotiable."

Poppy was trying to imagine Isaiah Grayson with a kitten living in his house. He had barn cats. And he had myriad horses and animals at his ranch, but he did not have a kitten. Though, because he already had so many animals, it was likely that he would be okay with one more.

"I will… Make a note of that."

"Oh," the woman continued. "I can also tie a cherry stem into a knot with my tongue."

Poppy closed her eyes and prayed for the strength to not run out of the room and hit Isaiah over the head with a wastebasket. "I assume I should mark that down under special skills."

"Men like that," the woman said.

Well, maybe that was why Poppy had such bad luck with men. She couldn't do party tricks with her tongue. In fairness, she'd never tried.

"Good to know," Poppy continued.

Poppy curled her hands into fists and tried to keep herself from... She didn't even know what. Screaming. Running from the room.

One of these women who she interviewed today might very well be the woman Isaiah Grayson slept with for the rest of his life. The last woman he ever slept with. The one who made him completely and totally unavailable to Poppy forever.

The one who finally killed her fantasy stone-cold.

She had known that going in. She had. But suddenly it hit her with more vivid force.

*I am your boss.*

Her boss. Her boss. He was her boss. Not her friend. Not her lover. Never her lover.

Maybe he didn't see his future wife as a new car he was buying. But he basically saw Poppy as a stapler. Efficient and useful only when needed.

"Well, I will be in touch," Poppy stated crisply.

"Why are *you* interviewing all the women? Is this like a sister wives thing?"

Poppy almost choked. "No. I am Mr. Grayson's assistant. Not his wife."

"I wouldn't mind that," Lola continued. "It's always seemed efficient to me. Somebody to share the workload of kids and housework. Well, and sex."

"Not. His. Wife." Poppy said that through clenched teeth.

"He should consider that."

She tightened her hold on her pen, and was surprised she didn't end up snapping it in half. "Me as his wife?"

"Sister wives."

"I'll make a note," Poppy said drily.

Her breath exited her body in a rush when Lola finally left, and Poppy's head was swimming with rage.

She had thought she could do this. She had been wrong. She had been an idiot.

*I am your boss.*

He was her boss. Because she worked for him. Because she had worked for him for ten years. Ten years.

Why had she kept this job for so long? She had job experience. She also had a nest egg. The money was good, she couldn't argue that, but she could also go get comparable pay at a large company in a city, and she now had the experience to do that. She didn't have to stay isolated here in Copper Ridge. She didn't have to stay with a man who didn't appreciate her.

She didn't have to stay trapped in this endless hell of wanting something she was never going to have.

No one was keeping her here. Nothing was keeping her here.

Nothing except the ridiculous idea that Isaiah had feelings for her that went beyond that of his assistant.

Friends could be friends in different cities. They didn't have to live in each other's pockets. Even if he had misspoken and he did see them as friends— and really, now that she was taking some breaths, she imagined that was closer to the truth—it was no excuse to continue to expose herself to him for twelve hours a day.

He was her business life. He was her social life. He was her fantasy life. That was too much for one man. Too much.

She walked into his office, breathing hard, and he looked up from his computer screen, his gray eyes assessing. He made her blood run hotter. Made her hands shake and her stomach turn over. She wanted him. Even now. She wanted to launch herself across the empty space and fling herself into his arms.

No. It had to stop.

"I quit," she said, the words tumbling out of her mouth in a glorious triumph.

But then they hit.

Hit him, hit her. And she knew she could take them back. Maybe she should.

No. She shouldn't.

"You *quit*?"

"It should not be in my job description to find you a wife. This is ludicrous. I just spent the last twenty minutes talking to a woman who was trying to get me to add the fact that she could tie a cherry stem into a knot with her tongue onto that ridiculous, awful form of yours underneath her '*skills*.'"

He frowned. "Well, that is a skill that might have interesting applications..."

"I know that," she said. "But why am I sitting around having a discussion with a woman that is obviously about your penis?"

Her cheeks heated, and her hands shook. She could not believe she had just... Talked about his penis. In front of him.

"I didn't realize that would be a problem."

"Of course you didn't. Because you don't realize *anything*. You don't care about anything except the bottom line. That's all you ever see. You want a wife to help run your home. To help organize your life. By those standards *I* have been your damned wife for the past ten years, Isaiah Grayson. Isn't that what you're after? A personal assistant for your house. A *me* clone who can cook your dinner and...and...do wife things."

He frowned, leaning back in his chair.

He didn't speak, so she just kept going. "I quit," she repeated. "And you have to find your own wife. I'm not working with you anymore. I'm not dealing with you anymore. You said you were my boss. Well, you're not now. Not anymore."

"Poppy," he said, his large, masculine hands pressing flat on his desk as he pushed himself into a standing position. She looked away from his hands.

They were as problematic as the rest of him. "Be reasonable."

"No! I'm not going to be reasonable. This situation is so unreasonable it isn't remotely fair of you to ask me to be reasonable within it."

They just stayed there for a moment, regarding each other, and then she slowly turned away, her breath coming in slow, harsh bursts.

"Wait," he said.

She stopped, but she didn't turn. She could feel his stare, resting right between her shoulder blades, digging in between them. "You're right. What I am looking for is a personal version of you. I hadn't thought about it that way until just now. But I am looking for a PA. In all areas of my life."

An odd sensation crept up the back of her neck, goose bumps breaking out over her arms. Still, she fought the urge to turn.

"Poppy," he said slowly. "I think you should marry me."

# Three

When Poppy turned around to face him, her expression was still. Placid. He wasn't good at reading most people, but he knew Poppy. She was expressive. She had a bright smile and a stormy frown, and the absence of either was...concerning.

"Excuse me?"

"You said yourself that what I need is someone like you. I agree. I've never been a man who aims for second best. So why would I aim for second best in this instance? You're the best personal assistant I've ever had."

"I doubt you had a personal assistant before you had me," she said.

"That's irrelevant," he said, waving a hand. "I

like the way we work together. I don't see why we couldn't make it something more. We're good partners, Poppy."

Finally, her face moved. But only just the slightest bit. "We're good partners," she echoed, the words hollow.

"Yes," he confirmed. "We are. We always have been. You've managed to make seamless transitions at every turn. From when we worked at a larger construction firm, to when we were starting our own. When we expanded, to when we merged with Jonathan Bear. You've followed me every step of the way, and I've been successful in part because of the confidence I have that you're handling all the details that I need you to."

"And you think I could just… Do that at your house too?"

"Yes," he said simply.

"There's one little problem," Poppy said, her cheeks suddenly turning a dark pink. She stood there just staring for a moment, and the color in her face deepened. It took her a long while to speak. "The problem being that a wife doesn't just manage your kitchen. *That* is a housekeeper."

"I'm aware of that."

"A wife is supposed to…" She looked down, a pink blush continuing to bleed over her dark skin. "You don't feel that way about me."

"Feel what way? You know my desire to get married has nothing to do with love and romance."

"Sex." The word was like a mini explosion in the room. "Being a wife does have something to do with sex."

She was right about that, and when he had made his impromptu proposal a moment earlier, he hadn't been thinking of that. But now that he was…

He took a leisurely visual tour of her, similar to the one he had taken earlier. But this time, he didn't just appreciate her beauty in an abstract sense. This time, he allowed it to be a slightly more heated exploration.

Her skin looked smooth. He had noticed how lovely it was earlier. But there was more than that. Her breasts looked about the right size to fit neatly into his hands, and she had an extremely enticing curve to her hips. Her skirts were never short enough to show very much of her leg, but she had nice ankles.

He could easily imagine getting down on his knees and taking those high heels off her feet. And biting one of her ankles.

That worked for him.

"I don't think that's going to be a problem," he said.

Poppy's mouth dropped open and then snapped shut. "We've never even… We've never even kissed, Isaiah. We've never even almost kissed."

"Yes. Because you're my assistant."

"Your assistant. And you're my foster sister's ex-fiancé."

Isaiah gritted his teeth, an involuntary spike of anger elevating his blood pressure. Poppy knew better than to talk about Rosalind. And hell, she had nothing to do with Poppy. Not in his mind, not anymore.

Yes, she was the reason Poppy had come to work for him in the first place, but Poppy had been with him for so long her presence wasn't connected with the other woman in any way.

He wasn't heartbroken. He never had been, not really. He was angry. She'd made a fool of him. She'd caused him to take his focus off his business. She'd nearly destroyed not only his work, but his brother's. And what would eventually be their sister's too.

All of it, all the success they had now had nearly been taken out by his own idiocy. By the single time he'd allowed his heart to control him.

He would never do that again.

"Rosalind doesn't have anything to do with this," he said.

"She's in my life," Poppy pointed out.

"That's a detail we can discuss later." Or not at all. He didn't see why they were coming close to discussing it now.

"You don't want to marry me," Poppy said.

"Are you questioning my decision-making, Poppy? How long have you known me? If there's one thing I'm not, it's an indecisive man. And I think you know that."

"You're a dick," Poppy said in exasperation. "How

dare you... Have me interviewing these women all day... And then... Is this some kind of sick test?"

"You threatened to quit. I don't *want* you to quit. I would rather have you in all of my life than in none of my life."

"I didn't threaten to quit our friendship."

"I mostly see you at work," he said.

"And you value what I do at work more than what you get out of our friendship, is that it?"

That was another question he didn't know how to answer. Because he had a feeling the honest answer would earn him a spiked heel to the forehead. "I'm not sure how the two are separate," he said, thinking he was being quite diplomatic. "Considering we spend most of our time together at work, and my enjoyment of your company often dovetails with the fact that you're so efficient."

Poppy let out a howl that would not have been out of place coming from an enraged chipmunk. "You are... You are..."

Well, if her objection to the marriage was that they had never kissed, and never almost kissed, and he didn't want to hear her talk anymore—and all those things were true—he could only see one solution to the entire situation.

He made his way over to where Poppy was standing like a brittle rose and wrapped his arms around her waist. He dragged her to him, holding her in place as he stared down at her.

"Consider this your almost-kiss," he said.

Her brown eyes went wide, and she stared up at him, her soft lips falling open.

And then his heart was suddenly beating faster, the unsettled feeling in his gut transforming into something else. Heat. Desire. He had never looked at Poppy this way, ever.

And now he wondered if that had been deliberate. Now he wondered if he had been purposefully ignoring how beautiful she was because of all the reasons she had just mentioned for why they shouldn't get married.

The fact she was his assistant. The fact that she was Rosalind's foster sister.

"Isaiah..."

He moved one hand up to cup her cheek and brought his face down closer to hers. She smelled delicate, like flowers and uncertainty. And he found himself drawn to her even more.

"And this will be your kiss."

He brought his lips down onto hers, expecting... He didn't know what.

Usually, sexual attraction was a straightforward thing for him. That was one of the many things he liked about sex. There was no guesswork. It was honest. There was never anything shocking about it. If he saw a woman he thought was beautiful, he approached her. He never wondered if he would enjoy kissing her. Because he always wanted to kiss her before he did. But Poppy...

In the split second before their mouths touched,

he wondered. Wondered what it would be like to kiss this woman he had known for so long. Who he had seen as essential to his life, but never as a sexual person.

And then, all his thoughts burned away. Because she tasted better than anything he could remember and her lips just felt right.

It felt equally right to slide his fingertips along the edge of her soft jawline and tilt her face up farther so he could angle his head in deep and gain access. It felt equally right to wrap both arms around her waist and press her body as tightly to his as he possibly could. To feel the soft swell of her breasts against his chest.

And he waited, for a moment, to see if she was going to stick her claws into him. To see if she was going to pull away or resist.

She did neither. Instead, she sighed, slowly, softly. Sweetly. She opened her mouth to his.

He took advantage of that, sliding his tongue between her lips and taking a taste.

He felt it, straight down to his cock, a lightning bolt of pleasure he'd had no idea was coming.

Suddenly, he was in the middle of a violent storm when only a moment ago the sky had been clear.

He had never experienced anything like it. The idea that Poppy—this woman who had been a constant in his world—was a hidden temptress rocked him down to his soul. He had no idea such a thing was possible.

In his world, chemistry had always been both straightforward and instant. That it could simply exist beneath the surface like this seemed impossible.

And yet, it appeared there was chemistry between himself and Poppy that had been dormant all this time.

Her soft hands were suddenly pressed against his face, holding on to him as she returned his kiss with surprising enthusiasm.

Her enthusiasm might be surprising, but he was damn well going to take advantage of it.

Because if chemistry was her concern, then he was more than happy to demolish her worry here and now.

He reversed their positions, turning so her back was to his desk, and then he walked her backward before sliding one arm beneath her ass and picking her up, depositing her on top of the desk. He bent down to continue kissing her, taking advantage of her shock to step between her legs.

Or maybe he wasn't taking advantage of anything. Maybe none of this was calculated as he would like to pretend that it was. Maybe it was just necessary. Maybe now that their lips had touched there was just no going back.

And hell, why should they? If she couldn't deny the chemistry between them… If it went to its natural conclusion…she had no reason to refuse his proposal.

He slid one hand down her thigh, toward her knee,

and then lifted that leg, hooking it over his hip as he drew her forward and pressed himself against her.

Thank God for the fullness of her skirt, because it was easy to make a space for himself right there between her legs. He was so hard it hurt.

He was a thirty-six-year-old man who had a hell of a lot more self-control now than he'd ever had, and yet, he felt more out of control than he could ever remember being before.

That did not add up. It was bad math.

And right now, he didn't care.

Slowly, he slid his other hand up and cupped her breast. He had been right. It was exactly the right size to fill his palm. He squeezed her gently, and Poppy let out a hoarse groan, then wrenched her mouth away from his.

Her eyes were full of hurt. Full of tears.

"Don't," she said, wiggling away from him.

"What?" he asked, drawing a deep breath and trying to gain control over himself.

Stopping was the last thing he wanted to do. He wanted to strip that dress off her, marvel at every inch of uncovered skin. Kiss every inch of it. He wanted her twisting and begging underneath him. He wanted to sink into her and lose himself. Wanted to make her lose herself too.

*Poppy.*

His friend. His assistant.

"How dare you?" she asked. "How dare you try to manipulate me with… wth *sex*. You're my friend,

Isaiah. I trusted you. You're just…trying to control
me the way you control everything in your life."

"That isn't true," he said. It wasn't. It might have
started out as…not a manipulation, but an attempt
to prove something to both of them.

But eventually, he had just been swept up in all
this. In her. In the heat between them.

"I think it is. You… I quit."

And then she turned and walked out of the room,
leaving him standing there, rejected for the first time
in a good long while.

And it bothered him more than he would have
ever imagined.

Poppy was steeped in misery by the time she
crawled onto the couch in her pajamas that evening.

Her little house down by the ocean was usually
a great comfort to her. A representation of security
that she had never imagined someone like her could
possess.

Now, nothing felt like a refuge. Nothing at all.
This whole town felt like a prison.

Her bars were Isaiah Grayson.

That had to stop.

She really was going to quit.

She swallowed, feeling sick to her stomach. She
was going to quit and sell this house and move away.
She would talk to him sometimes, but mostly she had
to let the connection go.

She didn't mean to him what he did to her. Not

just in a romantic way. Isaiah didn't... He didn't understand. He didn't feel for people the way that other people felt.

And he had used the attraction she felt for him against her. Her deepest, darkest secret.

There was no way a woman without a strong, pre-existing attraction would have ever responded to him the way she had.

It had been revealing. Though, now she wondered if it had actually been revealing at all, or if he had just always known.

Had he known—all this time—how much she wanted him? And had he been...laughing at her?

No. Not laughing. He wouldn't do that. He wasn't cruel, not at all. But had he been waiting until it was of some use to him? Maybe.

She wailed and dragged a blanket down from the back of the couch, pulling it over herself and curling into a ball.

She had kissed Isaiah Grayson today.

More than kissed. He had... He had touched her.

He had *proposed* to her.

And, whether it was a manipulation or not, she had felt...

He had been hard. Right there between her legs, he had been turned on.

But then, he was a man, and there were a great many men who could get hard for blowup dolls. So. It wasn't like it was that amazing.

Except, something about it felt kind of amazing.

She closed her eyes. Isaiah. He was… He was absolutely everything to her.

She could marry him. She could keep another woman from marrying him.

*Great. And then you can be married to somebody who doesn't love you at all. Who sees you as a convenience.*

She laughed aloud at that thought. Yes. Some of that sounded terrible. But… She had spent most of her life in foster care. She had lived with a whole lot of people who didn't love her. And some of them had found her to be inconvenient. So that would put marrying Isaiah several steps above some of the living situations she'd had as a kid.

Then there was Rosalind. Tall, blond Rosalind who was very clearly Isaiah's type. While Poppy was…not.

How would she ever…cope with that? With the inevitable comparisons?

*He hates her. He doesn't hate you.*

Well. That was true. Rosalind had always gone after what she wanted. She had devastated Isaiah in the process. So much so that it had even hurt Poppy at the time. Because as much as she wanted to be with Isaiah, she didn't want him to be hurt.

And then, Rosalind had gone on to her billionaire. The man she was still with. She traveled around the world and hosted dinner parties and did all these things that had been beyond their wildest fantasies when they were growing up.

Rosalind wasn't afraid of taking something just for herself. And she didn't worry at all about someone else's feelings.

Sometimes, that was a negative. But right about now... Poppy was tempted—more than a little bit tempted—to be like Rosalind.

To go after her fantasy and damn the feelings and the consequences. She could have him. As her husband. She could have him...kissing her. She could have him naked.

She could be *his*.

She had been his friend and his assistant for ten years. But she'd never been his in the way she wanted to be.

He'd been her friend and her boss.

He'd never been hers.

Had anyone ever been hers?

Rosalind certainly cared about Poppy, in her own way. If she didn't, she wouldn't have bailed Poppy out when she was in need. But Rosalind's life was very much about her. She and Poppy kept in touch, but that communication was largely driven by Poppy.

That was...it for her as far as family went. Except for the Graysons.

And if she married Isaiah...they really would be her family.

There was a firm, steady knock on her door. Three times. She knew exactly who it was.

It was like thinking about him had conjured him up.

She wasn't sure she was ready to face him.

She looked down. She was wearing a T-shirt and no bra. She was definitely not ready to face him. Still, she got up off the couch and padded over to the door. Because she couldn't *not*…

She couldn't not see him. Not right now. Not when all her thoughts and feelings were jumbled up like this. Maybe she would look at him and get a clear answer. Maybe she would look at him and think, *No, I still need to quit.*

Or maybe…

She knew she was tempting herself. Tempting him.

She hoped she was tempting him.

She scowled and grabbed hold of her blanket, wrapping it tightly around her shoulders before she made her way to the door. She wrenched it open. "What are you doing here?"

"I came to talk sense into you."

"You can't," she said, knowing she sounded like a bratty kid and not caring at all.

"Why not?"

"Because I am an insensible female." She whirled around and walked back into her small kitchen, and Isaiah followed her, closing the front door behind him.

She turned to face him again, and her heart caught in her throat. He was gorgeous. Those cold, clear gray eyes, his sculpted cheekbones, the beard that made him more approachable. Because without it, she had a feeling he would be too pretty. And his lips...

She had kissed those lips.

He was just staring at her.

"I'm emotional."

He said nothing to that.

"I might actually throw myself onto the ground at any moment in a serious display of said emotion, and you won't like it at all. So you should probably leave."

Those gray eyes were level with hers, sparking heat within her, stoking a deep ache of desire inside her stomach.

"Reconsider." His voice was low and enticing, and made her want to agree to whatever commandment he issued.

"Quitting or marrying you?" She took a step back from him. She couldn't be trusted to be too close to him. Couldn't be trusted to keep her hands to herself. To keep from flinging herself at him—either to beat him or kiss him she didn't know.

"Both. Either."

Just when she thought he couldn't make it worse.

"That's not exactly the world's most compelling proposal."

"I already know that my proposal wasn't all that compelling. You made it clear."

"I mean, I've heard of bosses offering to give a raise to keep an employee from leaving. But offering marriage..."

"That's not the only reason I asked you to marry me," he said.

She made a scoffing sound. "You could've fooled me."

"I'm not trying to fool you," he said.

Her heart twisted. This was one of the things she liked about Isaiah. It was tempting to focus on his rather grumpy exterior, and when she did that, the question of why she loved him became a lot more muddled. Because he was hot? A lot of men were hot. That wasn't it. There was something incredibly endearing about the fact that he said what he meant. He didn't play games. It simply wasn't in him. He was a man who didn't manipulate. And that made her accusation from earlier feel...wrong.

Manipulation wasn't really the right way to look at it. But he was used to being in charge. Unquestioned.

And he would do whatever he needed to do to get his way, that much she knew.

"Did you take the kiss as far as you did because you wanted to prove something to me?"

"No," he said. "I kissed you to try and prove something to *me*. Because you're right. If we were going to get married, then an attraction would have to be there."

"Yes," she said, her throat dry.

"I can honestly say that I never thought about you that way."

She felt like she'd just been stabbed through the chest with a kitchen knife. "Right," she said, instead of letting out the groan of pain that she was tempted to issue.

"We definitely have chemistry," he said. "I was genuinely caught off guard by it. I assume it was the same for you."

She blinked. He really had no idea? Did he really not know that her response to him wasn't sudden or random?

No. She could see that he didn't.

Isaiah often seemed insensitive because he simply didn't bother to blunt his statements to make them palatable for other people. Because he either didn't understand or care what people found offensive. Which meant, if backed into a corner about whether or not he had been using the kiss against her, he would have told her.

"I'm sorry," she said.

Now he looked genuinely confused. "You're apologizing to me. Why?"

"I'm apologizing to you because I assumed the worst about you. And that wasn't fair. You're not underhanded. You're not always sweet or cuddly or sensitive. But you're not underhanded."

"You like me," he pointed out.

He looked smug about that.

"Obviously. I wouldn't have put up with you for the past ten years. Good paying job or not. But then, I assume you like me too. At least to a degree."

"We're a smart match," he said. "I don't think you can deny that."

"Just a few hours ago you were thinking that one of those bottle blondes was your smart match. You can see why I'm not exactly thrilled by your sudden proposal to me."

"Are you in love with someone else?"

The idea was laughable. She hadn't even been on a date in…

She wasn't counting. It was too depressing.

"No," she said, her throat tightening. "But is it so wrong to want the possibility of love?"

"I think love is good for the right kind of people. Though my observation is that people mostly settle into a partnership anyway. The healthiest marriage is a partnership."

"Love is also kind of a thing."

He waved a hand. "Passion fades. But the way you support one another… That's what matters. That's what I've seen with my parents."

She stared at him for a long moment. He was right in front of her, asking for marriage, and she still felt like he was standing on the other side of a wall. Like she couldn't quite reach him. "And you're just…never going to love anyone."

"I *have* loved someone," he said simply.

There was something so incredibly painful about that truth. That he had loved someone. And she had used the one shot he was willing to give. It wasn't fair. That Rosalind had gotten his love. If Poppy would have had it, she would have preserved it. Held it close. Done anything to keep it for always.

But she would never get that chance. Because her vivacious older foster sister had gotten it first. And Rosalind hadn't appreciated what she'd had in him.

It was difficult to be angry at Rosalind over what had happened. Particularly when her and Isaiah being together had been painful for Poppy anyway. But right now… Right now, she was angry.

Because whole parts of Isaiah were closed off to Poppy because of the heartbreak he'd endured.

Or maybe that was silly. Maybe it was just going to take a very special woman to make him fall in love. And she wasn't that woman.

*Well, on the plus side, if you don't marry him, you'll give him a chance to find that woman.*

She clenched her teeth, closing her eyes against the pain. She didn't think she could handle that. It was one terrible thing to think about watching him marry another woman. But it was another, even worse thing to think about him falling in love with someone else. If she were good and selfless, pure and true, she supposed that's what she would want for him.

But she wasn't, and she didn't. Because if he fell in love, that would mean she wasn't going to get what she wanted. She would lose her chance at love. At least, the love she wanted.

How did it benefit her to be that selfless? It just didn't.

"I'll think about it," she said.

# Four

"I'm not leaving here until I close this deal," he said.

"I'm not a business deal waiting to happen, Isaiah."

He took a step toward her, and she felt her resolve begin to weaken. And then, she questioned why she was even fighting this at all.

He was the one driving this train. He always was.

Because she loved him.

Because he was her boss.

Because he possessed the ability to remain somewhat detached, and she absolutely did not.

She could watch him trying to calculate his next move. She could see that it was difficult for him to think of this as something other than a business deal.

No, she supposed that what Isaiah was proposing *was* a business deal. With sex.

"You can't actually be serious," she said.

"I'm always serious."

"I get that you think you can get married and make it not about...*feelings*. But it's... I can't get over the sex thing, Isaiah. I can't."

There were many reasons for that, not the least of which being her own inexperience. But she was not going to have that discussion with him.

"The kiss was good." He said it like that solved everything. Like it should somehow deal with all of her concerns.

"A kiss isn't sex," she said lamely. As if pointing out one of the most obvious things in the world would fix this situation.

"Do you think it's going to be a problem?"

"I think it's going to be weird."

Weird was maybe the wrong word. Terrifying.

Able to rip her entire heart straight out of her chest.

"You're fixating," he said simply. "Let's put a pin in the sex."

"You can't put a pin in the sex," she protested.

"Why can't I put a pin in the sex?"

"Because," she said, waving her hand in a broad gesture. "The sex is like the eight-hundred-pound gorilla in the room. In lingerie. It will not be ignored. It will not be...pinned."

"Put a pin in it," he reiterated. "Let's talk about

everything else that a marriage between the two of us could offer you."

She sputtered. "Could offer *me*?"

"Yes. Of course, I don't expect you to enter into an arrangement that benefits only me. So far, I haven't presented you with one compelling reason why marriage between the two of us would be beneficial to you."

"And you think that's my issue?"

"I think it's one issue. My family loves you. I appreciate that. Because I'm very close to my family. Anyone I marry will have to get along with my family. You already do. I feel like you love my family…"

She closed her eyes. Yes. She did love the Grayson family. She loved them so much. They were the only real, functional family she had ever seen in existence. They were the reason she believed that kind of thing existed outside the land of sitcoms. If it weren't for them, she would have no frame of reference for that kind of normalcy. A couple who had been together all those years. Adult children that loved their parents enough to try to please them. To come back home and visit. Siblings who worked together to build a business. Who cared for each other.

Loud, boisterous holiday celebrations that were warm and inviting. That included her.

Yes, the Grayson family was a big, fat carrot in all of this.

But what Isaiah didn't seem to understand was that he was the biggest carrot of all.

An inescapably sexual thought, and she had been asked to put a pin in the sex. But with Isaiah she could never just set the sex aside.

"You love my ranch," he said. "You love to come out and ride the horses. Imagine. You would already be sleeping there on weekends. It would be easy to get up and go for a ride."

"I love my house," she protested.

"My ranch is better," he said.

She wanted to punch him for that. Except, it was true.

His gorgeous modern ranch house with both rustic and modern details, flawlessly designed by his sister, was a feat of architectural engineering and design. There was not a single negative thing she could say about the place.

Set up in the mountains, with a gorgeous barn and horses and all kinds of things that young, day-dreamer Poppy would have given her right arm to visit, much less inhabit.

He had horses. And he'd taught her to ride a year earlier.

"And I assume you want children."

She felt like the wind had been knocked out of her. "I thought we weren't going to talk about sex."

"We're not talking about sex. We're talking about children."

"Didn't your parents tell you where babies come from?"

His mouth flattened into a grim line. "I will admit

there was something I missed when I was thinking of finding a wife through an ad."

She rolled her eyes. "Really?"

"Yes. I thought about myself. I thought about the fact that I wanted children in the abstract. But I did not think about what kind of mother I wanted my children to have. You would be a wonderful mother."

She blinked rapidly, fighting against the sting of sudden tears. "Why would you think that?"

"I know you. I've watched the way you took care of me and my business for the last ten years. The way you handle everything. The details in my professional life, Joshua and Faith's, as well. I've seen you with Joshua's son."

"I was basically raised by wolves," she pointed out. "I don't know anything about families."

"I think that will make you an even better mother. You know exactly what not to do."

She huffed out a laugh. "Disappearing into a heroin haze is a good thing to avoid. That much I know."

"You know more than that," he said. "You're good with people. You're good at anticipating what they want, what they need. You're organized. You're efficient."

"You make me sound like an app, Isaiah."

"You're warm and…and sometimes sweet. Though, not to me."

"You wouldn't like me if I were sweet," she pointed out.

"No. I wouldn't. But that's the other thing. You

know how to stand up to me." The sincerity on his face nearly killed her. "We would be good together."

He sounded so certain. And she felt on the opposite side of the world from certain.

This was too much. It really was. Too close to everything she had ever dreamed about—without one essential ingredient. Except... When had she really ever been allowed to dream?

She had watched so many other people achieve their dreams. While she'd barely allowed herself to imagine...

A life with Isaiah.

Children.

A family of her own.

Isaiah had simply been off-limits in her head all this time. It had made working with him easier. It had made being his friend less risky.

But he was offering her fantasy.

How could she refuse?

"Your parents can't know it's fake," she said.

"Are you agreeing?"

She blinked rapidly, trying to keep her tears back. "They can't know," she repeated.

"It's not fake," he said simply. "We'll have a real marriage."

"They can't know about the ad. They can't know that you just... Are hiring me for a new position. Okay?"

"Poppy..."

"They can't know you're not in love with me."

She would die. She would die of shame. If his wonderful, amazing parents who only ever wanted the best for their children, who most certainly wanted deep abiding love for Isaiah, were to know this marriage was an arrangement.

"It's not going to come up," he said.

"Good. It can't." Desperation clawed at her, and she wasn't really sure what she was desperate for. For him to agree. For him to say he had feelings for her. For him to kiss her. "Or it's off."

"Agreed."

"Agreed."

For a moment she thought he *was* going to kiss her again. She wasn't sure she could handle that. So instead, she stuck her hand out and stood there, staring at him. He frowned but took her offered hand, shaking it slowly.

Getting engaged in her pajamas and ending it with a handshake was not the romantic story she would need to tell his family.

He released his hold on her hand, and she thought he was going to walk away. But instead, he reached out and pulled her forward, capturing her mouth with his after all, a flood of sensation washing over her.

And then, as quickly as it began, the kiss ended.

"No. It's not going to be a problem," he said.

She expected him to leave then. He was supposed to leave. But instead, he dipped his head and kissed her again.

She felt dizzy. And she wanted to keep on kissing him. This couldn't be happening. It shouldn't be happening.

But they were engaged. So maybe this had to happen.

She didn't know this man, she realized as he let out a feral growl and backed her up against her wall. This was not the cool, logical friend she had spent all these years getting to know. This was...

Well, this was Isaiah as a man.

She had always known he was a man. Of course she had. If she hadn't, she wouldn't have been in love with him. Wouldn't have had so many fantasies about him. But she hadn't *really* known. Not like this. She hadn't known what it would be like to be the woman he wanted. Hadn't had any idea just how hot-blooded a man as detached and cool as he was on a day-to-day basis could be when sex was involved.

*Sex.*

She supposed now was the time to bring up her little secret.

But maybe this was just a kiss, maybe they weren't going to have sex.

He angled his head then, taking the kiss deeper. Making it more intense. And then he reached down and gripped the hem of her T-shirt, pulling it up over her head.

She didn't have a bra on underneath, and she was left completely exposed. Her nipples went tight as he looked at her, as those familiar gray eyes, so cold and rational most of the time, went hot.

He stared at her, his eyes glittering. "How did I not know?"

"How did you not know what?" Her teeth chattered when she asked the question.

Only then did she realize she was afraid this would expose her. Because while she could handle keeping her love for Isaiah in a little corner of her heart while she had access to his body—while she claimed ownership of him, rather than allowing some other woman to have him—she could not handle him knowing how she felt.

She'd had her love rejected too many times in her life. She would never subject herself to that again. Ever.

"How did I not know how beautiful you were?" He was absolutely serious, his sculpted face looking as if it was carved from rock.

She reached out, dragged her fingertips over his face. Over the coarse hair of his beard.

She could touch him now. Like this.

The kiss in his office had been so abrupt, so shocking, that while she had enjoyed it, she hadn't fully been able to process all that it meant. All the changes that came with it.

She didn't touch Isaiah like this. She didn't touch him ever.

And now… She finally could.

She frowned and leaned forward, pressing her lips slowly against his. They were warm, and firm, and she couldn't remember anything in the world feeling this wonderful.

Slowly, ever so slowly, she traced the outline of his bottom lip with her tongue.

She was tasting him.

Ten years of fantasies, vague and half-realized, and they had led here. To this. To him.

She slid her hands back, pushing them through his hair as she moved forward, pressing her bare breasts to his chest, still covered by the T-shirt he was wearing.

She didn't want anything between them. Nothing at all.

Suddenly, pride didn't matter.

She pulled away from him for a moment, and his eyes went straight down to her breasts again.

That would be her salvation. The fact that he was a man. That he was more invested in breasts than in feelings.

He was never going to see how she felt. Never going to see the love shining from her eyes, as long as he was looking at her body. And in this, in sex, she had the freedom to express everything she felt.

She was going to.

Oh, she was going to.

She wrapped her arms around his neck and pushed forward again, claiming his mouth, pouring everything, every fantasy, into that moment.

He growled, his arm wrapping around her waist like a steel band, the other one going down to her thighs as he lifted her up off the ground, pulling her against him. She wrapped her legs around his waist and didn't protest at all when he carried them both from the kitchen back toward her bedroom.

She knew exactly where this was going.

But it was time.

If she were totally, completely honest with herself, she knew why she hadn't done this before.

She was waiting for him.

She always had been.

A foolish, humiliating truth that she had never allowed herself to face until now. But it made pausing for consideration pointless.

She was going to marry him.

She was going to be with him.

There was nothing to think about.

There was a small, fragile bubble of joy in her chest, something she had never allowed herself to feel before. And it was growing inside her now.

She could have this. She could have him.

She squeaked when he dropped her down onto the bed and wrenched his shirt up over his head. She lay back, looking at him, taking in the fine, sculpted angles of his body. His chest was covered with just the right amount of dark hair, extending in a line down the center of his abs, disappearing beneath the waistband of his jeans.

She was exceptionally interested in that. And, for the first time, she hoped she was going to have those questions answered. That her curiosity would be satisfied.

He moved his hands to his belt buckle and reality began to whisper in her ear as he worked through the loops.

She didn't know why reality had showed up. It was her knee-jerk reaction to good things, she supposed.

In her life, nothing stayed good for long. Not for her. Only other girls got what they wanted.

The fact of the matter was, she wasn't his second choice after her much more beautiful foster sister.

She wasn't even his tenth choice.

She had come somewhere down the line of she-didn't-even-want-to-know-how-many bar hookups and the women who had been in her office earlier today.

On the list of women he might marry, Poppy was below placing an ad as a solution.

That was how much of a last resort she was.

*At least this time you're a resort at all. Does it really matter if you're the last one?*

In many ways, it didn't. Not at all.

Because she wanted to be chosen, even if she was chosen last.

He slowly lowered the zipper on his jeans and all of her thoughts evaporated.

Saved by the slow tug of his underwear, revealing a line of muscle that was almost obscene and a shadow of dark hair before he drew the fabric down farther and exposed himself completely, pushing his pants and underwear all the way to the floor.

She tried not to stare openmouthed. She had never seen a naked man in person before. And she had never counted on seeing Isaiah naked. Had dreamed about it, yes. Had fantasized about it, sure. But, she had never really imagined that it might happen.

"Now it's your turn," he said, his voice husky. Affected.

"I…"

She was too nervous. She couldn't make her hands move. Couldn't find the dexterity to pull her pajama pants down. And, as skills went, taking off pajama pants was a pretty easy one.

He took pity on her. He leaned forward, cupping her chin and kissing her, bringing himself down onto the bed beside her and pressing his large, warm palm between her shoulder blades, sliding his hand down the line of her back, just beneath the waistband of those pajamas. His hand was hot and enticing on her ass, and she arched her hips forward, his erection brushing against the apex of her thighs.

She gasped, and he kissed her, delving deep as he did, bringing his other hand around to cup her breast, his thumb sliding over her nipple, drawing it into an impossibly tight bud.

She pressed her hands against his chest, and just stared at them for a moment. Then she looked up at his face and back down at her hands.

She was touching his bare chest.

Isaiah.

It was undeniable.

He was looking down at her, his dark brows locked together, his expression as serious as it ever was, and it was just...*him*.

She slid her hands downward, watching as they traveled. Her mouth went dry when she touched those ab muscles, when her hands went down farther. She paused, holding out her index finger and tracing the indention that ran diagonally across his body, straight toward that place where he was most male.

She avoided touching him there.

She didn't know *how*.

But then, he took hold of her hand, curved his fingers around it and guided her right toward his erection.

She held back a gasp as he encouraged her to curl her fingers around his thick length.

He was so hot. Hot and soft and hard all at once. Then she looked back up, meeting his eyes, and suddenly, it wasn't so scary. Because Isaiah—a man who was not terribly affected by anything at all in the world, who seemed so confident in his ability to control everything around him—looked absolutely at a loss.

His forehead had relaxed, his eyes fluttering closed, his lips going slack. His head fell back. She squeezed him, and a groan rumbled in his chest.

Right now, she had the control, the power.

Probably for the first and only time in their entire relationship.

She had never felt anything like this before. Not ever.

A pulse began to beat between her legs, need swamping her. She felt hollow there, the slickness a telltale sign of just how much she wanted him too. But she didn't feel embarrassed about it. It didn't make her feel vulnerable. They were equals in this. It felt…exhilarating. Exciting. Right here in her little bed, it felt safe. To want him as much as she did.

How could it not, when he wanted her too?

Experimentally, she pumped her hand along his length, and he growled.

He was beautiful.

Everything she'd ever wanted. She knew he'd been made for her. This man who had captured her heart, her fantasies, from the moment she'd first met him.

But she didn't have time to think about all of that, because she found herself flipped onto her back, with Isaiah looming over her. In an easy movement, he reached between them and yanked off her pants and underwear.

He made space for himself between her legs, gripping his arousal and pressing it through her slick folds, the intimacy of the action taking her breath away, and then the intense, white-hot pleasure that assaulted her when he hit that perfect spot cleared her mind of anything and everything.

He did it again, and then released his hold on himself, flexing his hips against her. She gasped, grabbing his shoulders and digging her fingers into his skin.

His face was a study in concentration, and he cupped her breast, teasing her nipple as he continued to flex his hips back and forth across that sensitive bundle of nerves.

Something gathered low in her stomach, that hollow sensation between her legs growing keener…

And he didn't stop. He kept at it, teasing her nipple, and moving his hips in a maddening rhythm.

The tension within her increased, further and further until it suddenly snapped. She gasped as her climax overtook her, and he captured that sound of pleasure with his mouth, before drawing back and pressing the himself into the entrance of her body. And then, before she had a chance to tense up, he pressed forward.

The shocking, tearing sensation made her cry out in pain.

Isaiah's eyes clashed with hers.

"What the hell?"

# Five

Isaiah was trying to form words, but he was completely overtaken by the feel of her around his body. She was so tight. So wet. And he couldn't do anything but press his hips forward and sink even deeper into her in spite of the fact that she had cried out with obvious pain only a second before.

He should stop. But she was kissing him again. She was holding him against her as she moved her hips in invitation. As her movements physically begged him to stay with her.

Poppy was a virgin.

He should stop.

He *couldn't* stop.

He couldn't remember when that had ever happened to him before. He didn't know if it ever had. He was all about control. It was necessary for a man like him. He had to override his emotions, his needs.

Right now.

But she was holding him so tight. She felt…so good. He had only intended to give her a kiss before he left. And he *had* intended to go. But he'd been caught up…in her. Not in triumph over the fact that he had convinced her to marry him.

No, he had been caught up in *her*.

In the wonder of kissing her. Uncovering her. Exploring her in a way he had never imagined he might.

But he'd had no idea—none at all—that she was this inexperienced.

Poppy was brash. She gave as good as she got. She didn't shy away from anything. And she hadn't shied away from this either.

She still wasn't.

Her hands traveled down to cup his ass, and she tugged at him, as if urging him on.

"Isaiah," she whispered. "Isaiah, please."

And he had no choice but to oblige.

He moved inside her, slowly at first, torturing them both, and trying to make things more comfortable for her.

He had no idea how he was supposed to have sex with a damned virgin. He never had before.

He had a type. And Poppy was against that type in every single way.

But it seemed to be working just fine for him now.

She pressed her fingertips to his cheek, then pulled him down toward her mouth. She kissed him. Slow and sweet, and he forgot to have control.

He would apologize later. For going too fast. Too hard. But she kept making these sounds. Like she wanted it. Like she liked it. She wrapped her legs around his hips and urged him on, like she needed it. And he couldn't slow down. Couldn't stop. Couldn't make it better, even if he should.

He should make her come at least three more times before he took his own pleasure, but he didn't have the willpower. Not at all.

His pleasure overtook him, squeezing down on his windpipe, feeling like jaws to his throat, and he couldn't pull back. Not now. When his orgasm overtook him, all he could hear was the roar of his own blood in his ears, the pounding of his heartbeat. And then Poppy arched beneath him, her nails in his shoulders probably near to drawing blood as she let out a deep, intense cry, her internal muscles flexing around him.

He jerked forward, spilling inside her before he withdrew and rolled over onto his back. He was breathing hard, unable to speak. Unable to think.

"Poppy…"

"I don't want to talk about it," she said, crawling beneath a blanket beside him, covering herself up. She suddenly looked very small, and he was forced to sit there and do the math on their age difference.

It wasn't that big. Well, eight years. But he had never thought about what that might mean.

Of course, he had never known her to have a serious relationship. But then, he had only had the one, and he had certainly been having sex.

"We should talk about it."

"Why?" Her eyes were large and full of an emotion he couldn't grab hold of. But it echoed in him, and it felt a lot like pain. "There's really nothing to talk about. You know that my… My childhood was terrible. And I don't see why we have to go over all the different issues *that* might've given me."

"So you've been avoiding this."

It suddenly made sense why she had been so fixated on the sex aspect of his proposal. He'd been with a lot of women. So he had taken for granted that sex would be sex.

Of course, he had been wrong. He looked down at her, all vulnerable and curled into a ball. He kissed her forehead.

It hadn't just been sex. And of course poor Poppy had no reference at all for what sex would be like anyway.

"I'm sorry," he said.

"Don't be sorry. But I… I need to be alone."

That didn't sit well with him. The idea of leaving her like this.

"Please," she said.

He had no idea how to handle a woman in this state. Didn't know how to…

He usually wasn't frustrated by his difficulty connecting with people. He had a life that suited him. Family and friends who understood him. Who he knew well enough to understand.

Usually, he understood Poppy. But this was uncharted territory for the two of them, and he was at a loss for the right thing to do.

"If you really need that."

She nodded. "I do."

He got up, slowly gathering his clothes and walking out of the bedroom. He paused in her living room, holding those clothes in his hands. Then he dropped them. He lay down on her couch, which he was far too tall for, and pulled a blanket over himself.

There. She could be alone. In her room. And tomorrow they would talk. And put together details for their upcoming wedding.

He closed his eyes, and he tried not to think about what it had felt like to slide inside her.

But that was all he thought about.

Over and over again, until he finally fell asleep.

Poppy's eyes opened wide at three in the morning. She padded out into the hall, feeling disoriented. She was naked. Because she'd had sex with Isaiah last night.

And then she had sent him away.

Because… She didn't know why. She hated herself? She hated him? And everything good that could possibly happen to her?

She'd panicked. That was the only real explanation for her reaction.

She had felt stripped and vulnerable. She had wanted—needed—time to get a hold of herself.

Though, considering how she felt this morning, there probably wasn't enough time in the entire world for her to collect herself.

She had asked him to leave. And he'd left.

Of course he had.

She cared for that man with a passion, but he was not sensitive. Not in the least. Not even a little bit.

*You asked him to go. What do you want from him?*

It was silly to want anything but exactly what she had asked for. She knew it.

She padded out toward the living room. She needed something. A mindless TV show. A stiff drink. But she wasn't going to be able to go back to sleep.

When she walked into the living room, her heart jumped into her throat. Because there was a man-shaped something lying on her couch.

Well, it wasn't just man-shaped. It *was* a man.

Isaiah. Who had never left.

Who was defying her expectations again.

He'd been covered by a blanket, she was pretty sure, considering the fact that there was a blanket on the floor bunched up next to him. But he was still naked, sprawled out on her couch and now uncovered. He was...

Even in the dim light she could see just how incredible he was. Long limbs, strong muscles. So hard. Like he was carved from granite.

He was in many ways a mystery to her, even though she knew him as well as she knew anyone. If not better.

He was brilliant with numbers. His investments, his money management, was a huge part of what made Gray Bear Construction a success. He wasn't charismatic Joshua with an easy grin, good with PR and an expert way with people. He wasn't the fresh-faced wunderkind like Faith, taking the architecture world by storm with designs that outstripped her age and experience. Faith was a rare and unique talent. And Jonathan Bear was the hardest worker she had ever met.

And yet, Isaiah's work was what kept the company moving. He was the reason they stayed solvent. The reason that everything he had ever been involved with had been a success in one way or another.

But he was no pale, soft, indoor man. No. He was rugged. He loved spending time outdoors. Seemed to thrive on it. The moment work was through, Isaiah was out on his ranch. It amazed her that he had ever managed to live in Seattle. Though, even then, he had been hiking on the weekends, mountain biking and staying in cabins outside the city whenever he got the chance.

She supposed in many ways that was consistent enough. The one thing he didn't seem to have a perfect handle on was people. Otherwise, he was a genius.

But he had stayed with her.

In spite of the fact that she had asked him not to. She wasn't sure if that was an incredible amount of intuition on his part or if it was simply him being a stubborn ass.

"Are you just going to stand there staring at me?"

She jumped. "I didn't know you were awake."

"I wasn't."

"You knew I was looking at you," she said, shrinking in on herself slightly, wishing she had something to cover up her body.

Isaiah, for his part, looked completely unconcerned. He lifted his arms and clasped his hands, putting them behind his head. "Are you ready to talk?"

"I thought it was the woman who was supposed to be all needy and wanting to talk."

"Traditionally. Maybe. But this isn't normal for me. And I'm damn sure this isn't normal for you. You know, on account of the fact that you've never done this before."

"I said I didn't want to talk about my hymenal status."

"Okay."

He didn't say anything. The silence between them seemed to balloon, expand, becoming very, very uncomfortable.

"It wasn't a big deal," she said. "I mean, in that I

wasn't waiting for anything in particular. I was always waiting for somebody to care about me. Always. But then, when I left home… When I got my job with you…" She artfully left out any mention of Rosalind. "That was when I finally felt like I fit. And there just wasn't room for anything else. I didn't want there to be. I didn't need there to be."

"But now, with me, you suddenly changed your mind?"

She shifted, covering herself with her hand as she clenched her thighs more tightly together. "It's not that I changed my mind. I didn't have a specific No Sex Rule. I just hadn't met a man I trust, and I trust you and…and I got carried away."

"And that's never happened to you before," he said, keeping his tone measured and even. The way he handled people when he was irritated but trying not to show it. She knew him well enough to be familiar with that reaction.

"No," she admitted. Because there was no point in not telling him.

"You wanted this," he said, pushing into a sitting position. "You wanted it, didn't you?"

"Yes," she said. "I don't know how you could doubt that."

"Because you've never wanted to do this before. And then suddenly… You did. Poppy, I knew I was coercing you into marriage, but I didn't want to coerce you into bed."

"You didn't. We're engaged now anyway and…

It was always going to be you," she blurted out and then quickly tried to backtrack. "Maybe it was never going to happen for me if I didn't trust and know the person. But I've never had an easy time with trusting. With you, it just kind of...happened."

"Sex?"

"Trust."

"Come here."

"There?"

He reached out and took hold of her wrist, and then he tugged her forward, bringing her down onto his lap in an elegant tumble. "Yes."

He was naked. She was naked. She was sitting on his lap. It should feel ridiculous. Or wrong somehow. This sudden change.

But it didn't feel strange. It felt good.

He felt good.

"I'm staying," he said.

"I asked you to leave," she pointed out.

"You didn't really want me to."

"You can't know that," she said, feeling stubborn.

It really wasn't fair. Because she *had* wanted him to stay.

"Normally, I would say that's true. But I know you. And I knew that you didn't really want me to leave you alone *alone*."

"You knew that?"

"Yes, even I knew that," he said.

She lifted her hand, let it hover over his chest.

Then he took hold of it and pressed it down, over his heart. She could feel it thundering beneath her palm.

"I guess you can stay," she whispered.

"I'm too tall for this couch," he pointed out.

"Well, you can sleep on the floor."

That was when she found herself being lifted into the air as Isaiah stood. "I think I'll go back to your bed."

She swallowed, her heart in her throat, her body trembling. Were they really going to... Again?

"It's not a very comfortable bed," she said weakly.

"I think I can handle it."

Then he kissed her, and he kept on kissing her until they were back in her room.

Whatever desire she had to protect herself, to withdraw from him, was gone completely.

For the first time in her life, she was living her dream in Isaiah's arms. She wasn't going to keep herself from it.

# Six

Poppy was not happy when he insisted they drive to work together the next day.

But it was foolish for them to go separately. He was already at her house. She was clearly resisting him taking over every aspect of the situation, and he could understand that. But it didn't mean he could allow for impracticality.

Still, she threw him out of the bedroom, closed herself in and didn't emerge until it was about five minutes to the time they were meant to be there.

She was back in her uniform. A bright red skirt that fell down to her knees and a crisp, white top that she had tucked in. Matching red earrings and shoes added to the very Poppy look.

"Faith and Joshua are going to have questions," she said, her tone brittle as she got into the passenger seat of his sports car.

"So what? We're engaged."

"We're going to have to figure out a story. And... We're going to have to tell your parents. Your parents are not going to be happy if they're the last to know."

"We don't have to tell my siblings we're engaged."

"Oh, you just figure we can tell them we knocked boots and leave it at that?" Her tone told him she didn't actually think that was a good idea.

"Or not tell them anything. It's not like either of them keep me apprised of their sexual exploits."

"Well, Joshua is married and Faith is your little sister."

"And?"

"You are an endless frustration."

So was she, but he had a feeling if he pointed that out at the moment it wouldn't end well for him.

This wasn't a real argument. He'd already won. She was here with him, regardless of her protestations. He'd risk her wrath when it was actually necessary.

"Jonathan will not be in today, if that helps. At least, he's not planning on it as far as I know."

She made a noise halfway between a snort and clearing her throat. "The idea of dealing with Jonathan bothers me a lot less than dealing with your siblings."

"Well. We have to deal with them eventually.

There's no reason to wait. It's not going to get less uncomfortable. I could probably make an argument for the fact that the longer we wait the more uncomfortable we'll get."

"You know. If you could be just slightly less practical sometimes, it would make us mere mortals feel a whole lot better."

"What do you mean?"

"Everything is black-and-white to you. Everything is…easy." She looked like she actually meant that.

"That isn't true," he said. "Things are easy for me when I can line them out. When I can make categories and columns, so whenever I can do that, I do it. Life has variables. Too many. If you turn it into math, there's one answer. If the answer makes sense, go with that."

"But life *isn't* math," she said. "There's not one answer. We could hide this from everyone until we feel like not hiding it. We could have driven separate cars."

"Hiding it is illogical."

"Not when you're a woman who just lost her virginity and you're a little embarrassed and don't necessarily want everyone to know."

"You know," he said, his tone dry, "you don't have to walk in and announce that you just lost your virginity."

"I am aware of that," she snapped. She tapped her fingernails on the armrest of the passenger door.

"You know. You're a pretty terrible cowboy. What with the sports car."

"I have a truck for the ranch. But I also have money. So driving multiple cars is my prerogative."

She made a scoffing sound. And she didn't speak to him for the rest of the drive over.

For his part, Isaiah wasn't bothered by her mood. After she had come to speak to him in the early hours of the morning, he had taken her back to bed where he had kept her up for the rest of the night. She had responded to every touch, every kiss.

She might be angry at him, but she wanted him. And that would sustain them when nothing else would.

The whole plan was genius, really.

Now that they'd discovered this attraction between them, she really was the perfect wife for him. He liked her. She would be a fantastic mother. She was an amazing partner, and he already knew it. And then there was this…this heat.

It was more than he'd imagined getting out of a relationship.

So he could handle moments of spikiness in the name of all they had going for them.

They drove through the main street of town in silence, and Isaiah took stock of how the place looked, altered for Christmas. All the little shops adorned with strings of white lights and evergreen boughs.

It made him wonder about Poppy's life growing up. About the Christmases she might have had.

"Did you celebrate Christmas when you were a child?" he asked.

"What?"

"The Christmas decorations made me wonder. We did. Just…very normal Christmases. Like movies. A tree, family. Gifts and a dry turkey."

She laughed. "I have a hard time believing your mother ever made a dry turkey."

"My grandma made dry turkey," he said. "She died when I was in high school. But before then…"

"It sounds lovely," Poppy said. "Down to the dry turkey. I had some very nice Christmases. But there was never a routine. I also had years where there was no celebration. I don't have…very strong feelings about Christmas, actually. I don't have years of tradition to make into something special."

When they pulled into the office just outside of town, he parked, and Poppy wasted no time in getting out of the car and striding toward the building. Like she was trying to outrun appearing with him.

He shook his head and got out of the car, following behind her. Not rushing.

If she wanted to play a game, she was welcome to it. But she was the one who was bothered. Not him.

He walked into the craftsman-style building behind her, and directly into the front seating area, where his sister, Faith, was curled on a chair with her feet underneath her and a cup of coffee beside her.

Joshua was sitting in a chair across from her, his legs propped up on the coffee table.

"Are you having car trouble?" Faith directed that question at Poppy.

Poppy looked from Isaiah to Joshua and then to Faith. And he could sense when she'd made a decision. Her shoulders squared, her whole body became as stiff as a board, as if she were bracing herself.

She took a deep breath.

"No," she said. "I drove over with your brother because I had sex with him last night."

Then she swept out of the room and stomped down the hall toward her office. He heard the door slam decisively behind her.

Two heads swiveled toward him, wide eyes on his face.

*"What?"* his sister asked.

"I don't think she could have made it any clearer," he said, walking over to the coffeepot and pouring himself a cup.

"You had sex with Poppy," Joshua confirmed.

"Yes," Isaiah responded, not bothering to look at his brother.

"You… *You*. And Poppy."

"Yes," he said again.

"Why do I know this?" Faith asked, covering her ears.

"I didn't know she was going to make a pronouncement," Isaiah said. He felt a smile tug at his lips. "Though, she was kind of mad at me. So. I feel like this is her way of getting back at me for saying the change in our relationship was simple."

Faith's eyes bugged out. "You told her that it was simple. The whole thing. The two of you…*friends*… *Poppy*, an employee of the past ten years… *Sleeping together*." Faith was sputtering.

"It was good sex, Faith," he commented.

Faith's look contorted into one of abject horror, and she withdrew into her chair.

"There's more," Isaiah said. "I'm getting married to her."

"You are…*marrying Poppy*?" Now Faith was just getting shrill.

"Yes."

"You don't have to marry someone just because you have sex with them," Joshua pointed out.

"I'm aware of that, but you know I want to get married. And considering she and I have chemistry, I figured we might as well get married."

"But… Poppy?" Joshua asked.

"Why *not* Poppy?"

"Are you in love with her?" Faith asked.

"I care about her more than I care about almost anyone."

"You didn't answer my question," Faith said.

"Did no one respond to your ad?" Joshua was clearly happy to skip over questions about feelings.

Isaiah nodded. "Several women did. Poppy interviewed six of them yesterday."

Joshua looked like he wanted to say something that he bit back. "And you didn't like any of them?"

"I didn't meet any of them."

"So," Faith said slowly, "yesterday you had her interviewing women to marry you. And then last night you...hooked up with her."

"You're skipping a step. Yesterday afternoon she accused me of looking for a wife who was basically an assistant. For my life. And that was when I realized... She's actually the one I'm looking for."

"That is... The least romantic thing I've ever heard," Faith said.

"Romance is not a requirement for me."

"What about Poppy?"

He lifted a shoulder. "She could have said no."

*"Could she have?"* Faith asked. "I mean, no offense, Isaiah, but it's difficult to say no to you when you get something in your head."

"You don't want to hear this," Isaiah said, "but particularly after last night, I can say confidently that Poppy and I suit each other just fine."

"You're right," Faith said, "I don't want to hear it." She stood up, grabbing her coffee and heading back toward her office.

"I hope you know what you're doing," Joshua said slowly.

Isaiah looked over at his brother. "What about any of this doesn't look like I know what I'm doing?"

"Getting engaged to Poppy?" Joshua asked.

"You like Poppy," Isaiah pointed out.

"I do," Joshua said. "That's my concern. She's not like you. Your feelings are on a pretty deep freeze, Isaiah. I shouldn't have to tell you that."

"I don't know that I agree with you," he said.

"What's your stance on falling in love?"

"I've done it, and I'm not interested in doing it again."

"Has Poppy ever been in love before?" Joshua pressed.

Isaiah absolutely knew the answer to this question, not that it was any of his brother's business how he knew it. "No."

"Maybe she wants to be. And I imagine she wants her husband to love her."

"Poppy wants to be able to trust someone. She knows she can trust me. I know I can trust her. You can't get much better than that."

"I know you're anti-love… But what Danielle and I have…"

"What you and Danielle have is statistically improbable. There's no way you should have been able to place an ad in the paper for someone who is the antithesis of everything you should need in your life and fall madly in love with her. Additionally, I don't want that. I want stability."

"And my life looks terribly unstable to you?" Joshua asked.

"No. It doesn't. You forget, I was in a relationship for five years with a woman who turned out to be nothing like what I thought she was."

"You're still hung up on Rosalind?"

Isaiah shook his head. "Not at all. But I learned from my mistakes, Joshua. And the lesson there is that you can't actually trust those kinds of feelings. They blind you to reality."

"So you think I'm blind to reality?"

"And I hope it never bites your ass."

"What about Mom and Dad?"

"It's different," he said.

"How?"

"It's different for you too," Isaiah said. "I don't read people like you do. You know how to charm people. You know how to sense what they're feeling. How to turn the emotional tide of a room. I don't know how to do that. I have to trust my head because my heart doesn't give me a whole lot. What works for you isn't going to work for me."

"Just don't hurt her."

"I won't."

But then, Isaiah suddenly wasn't so sure. She was already hurt. Or at least, annoyed with him. And he wasn't quite sure what he was supposed to do about it.

He walked back toward Poppy's office and opened the door without knocking. She was sitting in her chair at her desk, not looking at anything in particular, and most definitely fuming.

"That was an unexpected little stunt," he said.

"You're not in charge of this," she pointed out. "If we are going to get married, it's a partnership. You don't get to manipulate me. You're not my boss in our marriage."

His lips twitched. "I could be your boss in the bedroom."

The color in her cheeks darkened. "I will allow that. However, in real life…"

"I get it."

He walked toward her and lowered himself to his knees in front of her, taking her chin in his hand. "I promise, I'm not trying to be a dick."

"Really?" He felt her tremble slightly beneath his touch.

He frowned. "I never try to be. I just am sometimes."

"Right."

"Joshua and Faith know. I mean, they already knew about the ad, and there was no way I was getting it by them that this wasn't related to that in some way."

"What did they say?"

"Joshua wants to make sure I don't hurt you."

She huffed a laugh. "Well. I'm team Joshua on that one."

"When do you want to tell my parents?" he asked. "We have our monthly dinner in three weeks."

"Let's…wait until then," she said.

"You want to wait that long?"

"Yes," she said. "I'm not…ready."

He would give her that. He knew that sometimes Poppy found interactions with family difficult. He'd always attributed that to her upbringing. "I understand. In the meantime, I want you to move your things into my house."

"But what about *my* house?" she asked.

"Obviously, you're coming to live on my ranch."

"No sex until we get married." The words came out fast and desperate.

He frowned. "We've already had sex. Several times."

"And that was…good. To establish our connection. It's established. And I want to wait now."

"Okay," he said.

She blinked. "Good."

He didn't think she'd hold to that. But Poppy was obviously trying to gain a sense of power here, and he was happy to give it to her.

Of course, that didn't mean he wouldn't try to seduce her.

# Seven

Poppy didn't have time to think much about her decision over the next few days. Isaiah had a moving company take all of her things to his house, and before she knew it, she was settling into a routine that was different from anything she had ever imagined she'd be part of.

They went to work together. They spent all day on the job, being very much the same Poppy and Isaiah they'd always been. But then they went home together.

And sexual tension seemed to light their every interaction on fire. She swore she could feel his body heat from across the room.

He had given her a room, her own space. But she could tell he was confused by her abstinence edict.

Even she was wondering why she was torturing herself.

Being with him physically was wonderful. But she felt completely overwhelmed by him.

She'd spent ten years secretly pining for him. Then in one moment, he'd decided he wanted something different, something more, and they'd been on their way to it. Isaiah had snapped his fingers and changed her world, and she didn't recognize even one part of it anymore.

Not even the ceiling she saw every morning when she opened her eyes.

She had to figure out a way to have power in this relationship. She was the one who was in love, and that meant she was at a disadvantage already. He was the one who got to keep his house. He was the one with the family she would become a part of.

She had to do something to hold on to her sanity.

It was hard to resist him though. So terribly hard.

When she felt lonely and scared at night, worrying for the future in a bedroom that was just down the hall from his, she wished—like that first night—that he would do a little less respecting of her commandments. That he would at least try to tempt her away from her resolve. Because if he did, she was sure it would fail.

But he didn't. So it was up to her to hang on to that edict.

No matter what.

Even when they had to behave like a normal couple for his parents' sakes.

And she was dreading the dinner at his parents' house tonight. With all of her soul.

Dreading having to tell a vague story about how they had suddenly realized their feelings for each other and were now making it official.

The fact that it was a farce hurt too badly.

But tonight they would actually discuss setting a wedding date.

A wedding date.

She squeezed her eyes shut for a moment, and then looked up at the gorgeous, custom-made cabinets in Isaiah's expansive kitchen. Maybe she should have a glass of wine before dinner. Or four. To calm her nerves.

She was already dressed and ready to go, but Isaiah had been out taking care of his horses, and she was still waiting for him to finish showering.

Part of her wished she could have simply joined him. But she'd made an edict and she should be able to stick to it.

She wondered if there was any point in preserving a sanity that was so frazzled as it was. Probably not.

Isaiah appeared a moment later, barefoot, in a pair of dark jeans with a button-up shirt. He was wearing his cowboy hat, looking sexy and disreputable, and exactly like the kind of guy who had been tailor-made for her from her deepest fantasies.

Or, maybe it was just that *he* was her fantasy.

Then he reached into his pocket and pulled out a black velvet box.

"No," she said.

He held it up. "No?"

"I didn't… I didn't know you were going to…"

"You have to have a ring before we see my parents."

"But then I'm going to walk in with a ring and they're going to know." As excuses went, it was a weak one. They were going to inform his parents of their engagement anyway.

They were engaged.

It was so strange. She didn't feel engaged to him. *Maybe because you won't sleep with him?*

*No. Because he doesn't love me.*

She had a snotty response at the ready for her internal critic. Because really.

"They won't know you're engaged to me. And even so, were not trying to make it a surprise. We're just telling them in person."

The ring inside the box was stunning. Ornately designed, rather than a simple solitaire.

"It's vintage," he said. "It was part of a museum collection, on display in Washington, DC. I saw it online and I contacted the owner."

"You bought a vintage ring out of a museum." It wasn't a question so much as a recitation of what he'd just said.

"It was a privately owned collection." As if that

explained it. "What?" he asked, frowning after she hadn't spoken for a few moments. "You don't look happy."

She didn't know how to describe what she was feeling. It was the strangest little dream come true. Something she would never have even given a thought to. Ever. She never thought about what kind of engagement ring she might want. And if she had, she would have asked for something small, and from the mall. Not from...*a museum collection.*

"I know how much you like vintage. And I know you don't like some of the issues surrounding the diamond trade."

She had gone on a small tirade in the office after seeing the movie *Blood Diamond* a few years ago. Just once. It wasn't like it was a cause she talked about regularly. "You...listened to that?"

"Yes," he responded.

Sometimes she wondered if everybody misunderstood him, including her. If no one knew just how deeply he held on to each moment. To people. Remembering a detail like that wasn't the mark of an unemotional man. It seemed...remarkably sentimental for him to remember such a small thing about her. Especially something that—at the time—wouldn't have been relevant to him.

She saw Isaiah as such a stark guy. A man who didn't engage in anything unnecessary. Or hold on to anything he didn't need to hold on to.

But that was obviously just what he showed the world. What he showed her.

It wasn't all of him.

It was so easy to think of him as cold, emotionless. He would be the first person to say a relationship could be a math equation for him, after all.

But remembering her feelings on diamonds wasn't math. It was personal.

There was no other man on earth—no other person on earth—who understood her the way Isaiah Grayson did.

She hadn't realized it until this moment. She'd made a lot of accusations about him being oblivious, but she was just as guilty.

And now…

She wanted to wear his ring. The ring he'd chosen for her with such thought and…well, extravagance. Because who had ever given her that kind of thought before? No one.

And certainly no one had ever been so extravagant for her.

Only him.

Only ever him.

He walked over to where she was sitting and took the ring out of the box, sliding it onto her finger. He didn't get down on one knee. But then, that didn't surprise her.

More to the point, it didn't matter.

The ring itself didn't even matter. It was the thought.

It was the man.

Her man.

It was how much she wanted it that scared her. That was the real problem. She wanted to wear his ring more than she wanted anything in the world.

And she was going to take it.

"Are you ready to go to dinner?"

She swallowed hard, looking down at the perfect, sparkly rock on her finger.

"Yes," she said. "I'm ready."

Isaiah felt a sense of calm and completion when they pulled into his parents' house that night. The small, modest farmhouse looked the same as it ever did, the yellow porch light cheery in the dim evening. It was always funny to him that no matter how successful Devlin, Joshua, Faith or Isaiah became, his parents refused to allow their children to buy them a new house. Or even to upgrade the old one at all.

They were perfectly happy with what they had.

He envied that feeling of being content. Being so certain what home was.

He liked his house, but he didn't yet feel the need to stop changing his circumstances. He wasn't settled.

He imagined that this new step forward with Poppy would change that. Though, he would like it if she dropped the sex embargo.

He wasn't quite sure why she was so bound by it, though she had said something about white weddings and how she was a traditional girl at heart, even though he didn't believe any of it since she had happily jumped into bed with him a few weeks earlier.

It was strange. He'd spent ten years not having sex with Poppy. But now that they'd done it a few times, it was damn near impossible to wait ten days, much less however long it was going to be until their wedding. He was fairly confident she wouldn't stick to her proclamation that whole time, though. At least, he had been confident until nearly three weeks had passed without her knocking on his bedroom door.

But then, Poppy had been a twenty-eight-year-old virgin. Her commitment to celibacy was much greater than his own. He might have spent years abstaining from relationships, but he had not abstained from sex.

They got out of the car, and she started to charge ahead of him, as she had done on the way into the office that first morning after they'd made love. He was not going to allow that this time.

He caught up with her, wrapping his arm around her waist. "If you walk into my parents' living room and announce that we had sex I may have to punish you."

She turned her head sharply, her eyes wide. "Punish me? What sort of caveman proclamation is that?"

"Exactly the kind a bratty girl like you needs if you're plotting evil."

"I'm *not* plotting evil," she said, her cheeks turning pink.

He examined her expression closely. Knowing Poppy like he did, he could read her better than he could read just about anyone else. She was annoyed with him. They certainly weren't back on the same footing they had been.

But she wanted him. She couldn't hide that, even now, standing in front of his parents' home.

"But you're a little bit intrigued about what I might do," he whispered.

She wiggled against him, and he could tell she absolutely, grudgingly was intrigued. "Not at all."

"You're a liar."

"You have a bad habit of pointing that out." She sounded crabby about that.

"I don't see the point of lies. In the end, they don't make anything less uncomfortable."

"Most people find small lies a great comfort," she disagreed.

"I don't," he said, a hot rock lodging itself in his chest. "I don't allow lies on any level, Poppy. That, you do have to know about me."

He'd already been in a relationship with a woman who had lied to him. And he hadn't questioned it. Because he'd imagined that love was somehow the same as having two-way trust.

"I won't lie to you," she said softly, brushing her fingertips over his lips.

Instantly, he felt himself getting hard. She hadn't touched him in the weeks since he'd spent the night in her bed. But now was not the time.

He nodded once, and then tightened his hold on her as they continued to walk up the porch. Then he knocked.

"Why do you knock at your parents' house?"

"I don't live here."

The door opened, and his mother appeared, looking between the two of them, her eyes searching.

"Isaiah? Poppy."

"Hi," Poppy said, not moving away from his hold.

"Hi, Mom," Isaiah said.

"I imagine you have something to tell us," his mom said, stepping away from the door.

Isaiah led Poppy into the cozy room. His father was sitting in his favorite chair, a picture of the life he'd had growing up still intact. The feeling it gave him… It was the kind of life he wanted.

"We have something to tell you," Isaiah said.

Then the front door opened again and his brother Devlin and his wife, Mia, who was heavily pregnant, walked into the room.

"We brought chips," Mia said, stopping cold when she saw Isaiah and Poppy standing together.

"Yay for chips," Poppy said.

Then Joshua, Danielle and baby Riley came in, and with the exception of Faith, the entire audience was present.

"Do you want to wait for Faith?" his mom asked.

"No," Isaiah said. "Poppy and I are engaged."

His mother and father stared at them, and then his

mother smiled. "That's wonderful!" She closed the distance between them and pulled him in for a hug.

She did the same to Poppy, who was shrinking slightly next to him, like she was her wilting namesake.

His father made his way over to them and extended his hand; Isaiah shook it. "A good decision," his dad said, looking at Poppy. And then, he hugged her, kissing her on the cheek. "Welcome to the family, Poppy."

Poppy made a sound that was somewhere between a gasp and a sob, but she stayed rooted next to his side.

This was what he wanted. This feeling. There was warmth here. And it was easy. There was closeness.

And now that he had Poppy, it was perfect.

Poppy didn't know how she made it through dinner. The food tasted like glue, which was ridiculous, since Nancy Grayson made the best food, and it always tasted like heaven. But Poppy had a feeling that her taste buds were defective, along with her very soul. She felt…wonderful and awful. All at once.

The Graysons were such an amazing family, and she loved Isaiah's parents. But they thought Isaiah and Poppy were in love. They thought Isaiah had finally shared his heart with someone.

And he didn't understand their assumptions. He thought they wanted marriage for him. A traditional family. But that wasn't really what they wanted.

They wanted his happiness.

And Isaiah was still… He was still in the same place he had always been, emotionally. Unwilling to open up. Unwilling to take a risk because it was so difficult. They thought she'd changed him, and she hadn't.

She was…enabling him.

She was enabling him and it was terrible.

After dinner, Poppy helped Nancy clear the dishes away.

"Poppy," she said. "Can I talk to you?"

Poppy shifted. "Of course."

"I've always known you would be perfect for him," Nancy said. "But I'm hesitant to push Isaiah into anything because he just digs in. They're all like that to a degree… But he's the biggest puzzle. He always has been. Since he was a boy. Either angry and very emotional, or seemingly emotionless. I've always known that wasn't true. People often find him detached, but I think it's because he cares so much."

Poppy agreed, and it went right along with what she'd been thinking when he'd given her the ring. That there were hidden spaces in him he didn't show anyone. And that had to be out of protection. Which showed that he did feel. He felt an awful lot.

"He's a good man," Nancy continued. "And I think he'll be a good husband to you. I'm just so glad you're going to be the one to be his wife, because you are exactly what he needs. You always have been."

"I don't… He's not difficult." Poppy looked down

at her hands, her throat getting tight. "He's one of the most special people I know."

Nancy reached out and squeezed Poppy's hands. "That's all any mother wants the wife of her son to think."

Poppy felt even more terrible. Like a fraud. Yes, she would love Isaiah with everything she had, but she wasn't sure she was helping him at all.

"I have something for you," Nancy said. "Come with me."

She led Poppy back to the master bedroom, the only room in the house Poppy had never gone into. Nancy walked across the old wooden floor and the threadbare braided rug on top, moving to a highboy dresser and opening up a jewelry box.

"I have my mother's wedding band here. I know that you like…old-fashioned things. It didn't seem right for Danielle. And I know Faith won't want it. You're the one it was waiting for." Nancy turned, holding it out to Poppy.

Poppy swallowed hard. "Thank you," she said. "I'll save it until the… Until the wedding."

"It can stay here, for safekeeping, if you want."

"If you could," Poppy said. "But I want to wear it. Once Isaiah and I are married." Married. She was going to marry Isaiah. "Thank you."

Nancy gave Poppy another hug, and Poppy felt like her heart was splintering. "I know that your own mother won't be at the wedding," Mrs. Grayson said. "But we won't make a bride's side and a groom's side. It's just going to be our family. You're our family now, Poppy. You're not alone."

"Thank you," Poppy said, barely able to speak.

She walked back out into the living room on numb feet to find Isaiah standing by the front door with his hat on. "Are you ready to go?" he asked.

"Yes," she said.

She got another round of hugs from the entire family, each one adding weight to her already burdened conscience.

When they got out, they made their way back to the car, and as soon as he closed the door behind them, Poppy's insides broke apart.

They pulled out of the driveway, and a tear slid down her cheeks, and she turned her face away from him to keep him from seeing.

"I can't do this."

# Eight

"What?"

"I can't do this," she said, feeling panic rising inside her now. "I'm sorry. But your parents think that I've...transformed you in some way. That I'm healing you. And instead, I'm enabling you to keep on doing that thing you love to do, where you run away from emotion and make everything about..."

"Maybe I just don't feel it," he said. "Maybe I'm not running from anything because there isn't anything there for me to run from. Why would you think differently?"

"Because you loved Rosalind..."

"Maybe. Or maybe I didn't. You're trying to make

it seem like I feel things the exact same way other people do, and that isn't fair. I don't."

"I'm not trying to. It's just that your parents think—"

"I don't give a damn what my parents think. You were the one who wanted them to believe this was a normal kind of courtship. I don't care either way."

"Of course you don't."

"This is ridiculous, Poppy. You can't pull out of our agreement now that everybody knows."

"I could," she said. "I could, and I could quit. Like I was going to do."

"Because you would find it so easy to leave me?"

"No!"

"You're doing this because you feel guilty? I don't believe it. I think you're running away. You accuse me of not dealing with my feelings. But you were a twenty-eight-year-old virgin. You've refused to let me touch you in the time since we first made love, and now that you've had to endure hugs from my entire family suddenly you're trying to escape like a feral cat."

"I am not a feral cat." The comparison was unflattering.

And a little bit too close to the truth.

"I think you are. I think you're fine as long as somebody leaves a can of tuna for you out by the Dumpster, but the minute they try to bring you in the house you're all claws and teeth."

"No one has ever left me a can of tuna by a Dumpster." If he wanted claws, she was on the verge of giving them to him. This entire conversation was getting ridiculous.

"This isn't over." He started to drive them back toward his house.

"It is," she protested.

"No."

"Take me back to *my* house," she insisted.

"My house *is* your house. You agreed to marry me."

"And now I'm *un*agreeing," she insisted.

"And I think you're full of shit," he said, his tone so sharp it could have easily sliced right through her. "I think you're a hypocrite. Going on about what I need to do. Worrying about my emotional health when your own is in a much worse place."

She huffed, clenching her hands into fists and looking away from him. She said nothing for the rest of the drive, and then when they pulled up to the house, Isaiah was out of the car much quicker than she was, moving over to her side and pulling open the door. Then he reached into the car, unbuckled her and literally lifted her out as though she were a child. Holding her in his arms, he carried her up the steps toward the house.

"What the hell are you doing?" she shouted.

"What I should have done weeks ago."

"Making the transformation from man to caveman complete?"

He slid his hand down toward her ass and heat

rioted through her. Even now, when she should be made of nothing but rage, she responded to him. Dammit.

"Making you remember why we're doing this."

"For your convenience," she hissed.

"Because I can't want another woman," he said, his voice rough, his eyes blazing. "Not now. And we both know you don't want another man."

She made a poor show of kicking her feet slightly as he carried her inside. She could unman him if she wanted to, but she wouldn't. And they both knew it.

"You can't do this," she protested weakly. "It violates all manner of HR rules."

"Too bad for you that I own the company. I *am* HR."

"I'm going to organize an ethics committee," she groused.

"This is personal business. The company has nothing to do with it."

"Is it? I think it's business for you, period, like everything else."

"It's personal," he ground out, "because I've been inside you. Don't you dare pretend that isn't true. Though it all makes sense to me now. Why you wanted me to stay away from you for the past few weeks."

"Because I'm just not that into you?" she asked as he carried her up the stairs.

"No. Because you're *too* into it."

She froze, ice gathering at the center of her chest.

She didn't want him to know. He had been so clueless up until this point.

"You're afraid that I'll be able to convince you to stay because the sex is so good."

Okay. Well, he was a little bit onto it. But not really.

Just a little bit off base, was her Isaiah.

"You're in charge of everything," she said. "I didn't think it would hurt you to have to wait."

"I don't play games."

"Sadly for you, the rest of the world does. We play games when we need to. We play games to protect ourselves. We play games because it's a lot more palatable than wandering around making proclamations like you do."

"I don't understand games," he said. He flung open the door to his bedroom and walked them both inside. "But I understand this." He claimed her mouth. And she should have… She should have told him no. Because of course he would have stopped. But she didn't.

Instead, she let him consume her.

Then she began to consume him back. She wanted him. That was the problem. As much as everything that had happened back at the Grayson house terrified her, she wanted him.

Terrified. That wasn't the word she had used before. Isaiah was the one who had said she was afraid. And maybe she was. But she didn't know what to do about it.

It was like the time she had gone to live with a couple who hadn't been expecting a little girl as young as she was. They had been surprised, and clearly, their house hadn't been ready for a boisterous six-year-old. There had been a list of things she wasn't allowed to touch. And so she had lived in that house for all of three weeks, afraid to leave feet print on the carpet, afraid of touching breakable objects. Afraid that somehow she was going to destroy the beautiful place she found herself in simply because of who she was.

Because she was the wrong fit.

That was what it had felt like at the Graysons' tonight. Like she was surrounded by all this lovely, wonderful love, and somehow, it just wasn't for her. Wasn't to be.

There was more to it than that, of course, but that was the *real* reason she was freaking out, and she knew it.

But it didn't make her *wrong*.

It also didn't make her want to stop what was happening with Isaiah right now.

She was lonely. She had been a neglected child, and then she had lived in boisterous houses full of lots of children, which could sometimes feel equally lonely. She had never had a close romantic relationship as an adult. She was making friends in Copper Ridge, but moving around as often as she had made it difficult for her to have close lifelong friends. Isaiah was that friend, essentially.

And being close to him like this was a balm for a wound that ran very, very deep.

"You think this is fake?" he asked, his voice like gravel.

He bent down in front of her, grabbing hold of her skirt and drawing it down her legs without bothering to take off her shoes. Her shirt went next.

"Sit down," he commanded, and her legs were far too weak to disobey him. He looked up at her, those gray eyes intent on hers. "Take your bra off for me."

With shaking hands, she found herself obeying him.

"I imagine you're going to report me to HR for this too." The smile that curved his lips told her he didn't much care.

"I might," she responded, sliding her bra down her arms and throwing it onto the floor.

"Well, then I might have to keep you trapped here so you can't tell anyone."

"This is a major infraction."

"Maybe. But then again. I am the boss. I suppose I could choose to reprimand you for such behavior."

"I… I suppose you could."

"You're being a very bad girl," he said, hooking his fingers in the waistband of her panties and pulling them down to her knees. "Very bad."

Panic skittered in her stomach, and she had no idea how to respond. To Isaiah being like this, so playful. To him being like this and also staring at her right where he was staring at her.

"You need to remember who the boss is," he said, moving his hands around her lower back and sliding them down to cup her ass. Then he jerked her forward, and she gasped as he pressed a kiss to the inside of her thigh.

Then he went higher, and higher still, while she trembled.

She couldn't believe he was about to do this. She wanted him to. But she was also scared. Self-conscious. Excited. It was a whole lot of things.

But then, everything with Isaiah was a lot.

He squeezed her with both hands and then moved his focus to her center, his tongue sliding through her slick folds. She clapped her hand over her mouth to keep from making an extremely embarrassing noise, but she had a feeling he could still hear it, muffled or not.

Because he chuckled.

Isaiah, who was often humorless, chuckled with his mouth where it was, and his filthy intentions were obvious even to her.

And then he started to show her what he meant by punishment. He teased her with his tongue, with his fingers, with his mouth. He scraped her inner thigh with the edge of his teeth before returning his attention to where she was most needy for him. But every time she got close he would back off. He would move somewhere else. Kiss her stomach, her wrist, her hand. He would take his attention off of exactly where she needed him.

"Please," she begged.

"Bad girls don't get to come," he said, the edge in his voice sharp like a knife.

Those words just about pushed her over the edge all on their own.

"I thought you said you didn't play games," she choked out.

"Let me rephrase that," he said, looking up at her, a wicked smile curving his mouth. "I only play games in the bedroom."

He pressed two fingers into her before laughing at her again with his tongue, taking her all the way to the edge again before backing off. He knew her body better than she did, knew exactly where to touch her, and where not to. Knew the exact pressure and speed. How to rev her up and bring her back.

He was evil, and in that moment, she felt like she hated him as much as she had ever loved him.

"Tell me what you want," he said.

"You *know*."

"I do," he responded. "But you have to tell me."

"You're mean," she panted.

"I'm a very, very mean man," he agreed, sounding unrepentant as he slid one finger back through her folds. Tormenting. Teasing. "And you like it."

"I don't," she insisted.

"You do. Which is your real problem with all of this. You want me. And you want this. Even though you know you probably shouldn't."

"Well, what about you?" she asked, breathing

hard. "You want it too. Or you wouldn't be trying so hard to convince me to go through with this marriage. Maybe *you* should beg."

"I'm on my knees," he said. "Isn't that like begging?"

"That's not—"

But she was cut off because his lips connected with that most sensitive part of her again. She could do nothing but feel.

She was so wet, so ready for him, so very hollow and achy that she couldn't stand for him to continue. It was going to kill her.

Or she was going to kill him. One of the two.

"Tell me," he whispered in her ear. "Tell me what you want."

"You," she said.

"Me?"

"You. Inside me. Please."

She didn't have to ask him twice.

Instead, she found herself being lifted up, brought down onto the bed, sitting astride him. He maneuvered her so her slick entrance was poised just above his hardness. And then he thrust up, inside her.

She gasped.

"You want to be in charge? Go ahead."

It was a challenge. And it gave her anything but control, when she was so desperate for him, when each move over him betrayed just how desperate she was.

He knew it too. The bastard.

But she couldn't stop, because she was so close, and now that she was on top she could...

Stars exploded behind her eyes, her internal muscles pulsing, her entire body shaking as her orgasm rocked her. All it had taken was a couple of times rocking back and forth, just a couple of times applying pressure where it was needed.

He growled, flipping her over and pinning her hands above her head. "You were just a bit too easy on me."

He kissed her then, and it was like a beast had been unleashed inside him. He was rough and untamed, and his response called up desire inside her again much sooner than she would have thought possible.

But it was Isaiah.

And with him, she had a feeling it would always be like this.

*Always?*

She pushed that mocking question aside.

She wasn't going to think about anything beyond this, right now.

She wasn't going to think about what she had told him before he carried her upstairs. About what she believed she deserved or didn't, about what she believed was possible and wasn't.

She was just going to feel.

This time, when the wave broke over her, he was swept up in it too, letting out a hoarse growl as he found his own release.

And when it was over, she didn't have the strength to get up. Didn't have the strength to walk away from him.

Tomorrow. Tomorrow would sort itself out.

Maybe for now she could hang on to the fantasy.

Poppy woke up in the middle of the night, curled around Isaiah's body. Something strange had woken her, and it wasn't the fact that she was sharing a bed with Isaiah.

It wasn't the fact that her resolve had weakened quite so badly last night.

There was something else.

She couldn't think what, or why it had woken her out of a dead sleep. She rolled away from him and padded into the bathroom that was just off his bedroom. She stood there for a moment staring at the mirror, at the woman looking back at her. Who was disheveled and had raccoon eyes because she hadn't taken her makeup off before allowing Isaiah to rock her world last night.

And then it suddenly hit her.

Because she was standing in a bathroom and staring at the mirror, and it felt like a strange kind of déjà vu.

It was the middle of the month. And she absolutely should've started her period by now.

She was two days late.

And she and Isaiah hadn't used a condom.

"No," she whispered.

It was too coincidental.

She went back into the bedroom and dressed as quickly and quietly as possible. And then she grabbed her purse and went downstairs.

She had to know.

She wouldn't sleep until she did. There were a few twenty-four-hour places in Tolowa, and she was going over there right now.

And that was how, at five in the morning in a public restroom, Poppy Sinclair's life changed forever.

# Nine

When Isaiah woke up the next morning, Poppy wasn't in bed with him. He was irritated, but he imagined she was still trying to hold on to some semblance of control with her little game.

She was going to end up agreeing to marry him. He was fairly confident in that. But what he'd said about her being like a stray cat, he'd meant. She might not like the comparison, but it was true enough. Now that he wanted to domesticate her, she was preparing to run.

But her common sense would prevail. It didn't benefit her *not* to marry him.

And she couldn't deny the chemistry between them. He wasn't being egotistical about that. What they had between them was explosive. It *couldn't* be denied.

When he got downstairs, he saw Poppy sitting at the kitchen table. She was dressed in the same outfit she'd been wearing last night, and she was staring straight ahead, her eyes fixed on her clenched fists.

"Good morning," he said.

"No, it isn't," she responded. She looked up at him, and then she frowned. "Could you put a shirt on?"

He looked down at his bare chest. He was only wearing a pair of jeans. "No."

"I feel like this is a conversation we should have with your shirt on." She kept her gaze focused on the wall behind him.

He crossed his arms over his chest. "I've decided I like the conversations I have with you without my shirt better."

"I'm not joking around, Isaiah."

"Then you don't have time for me to go get a shirt. What's going on?"

"I'm pregnant." She looked like she was delivering the news of a death to him.

"That's…" He let the words wash over him, took a moment to turn them over and analyze what they made him feel. He felt…calm. "That's good," he said.

*"Is it?"* Poppy looked borderline hysterical.

"Yes," he said, feeling completely confident and certain now. "We both want children."

It was sooner than he'd anticipated, of course,

but he wanted children. And…there was something relieving about it. It made this marriage agreement feel much more final. Made it feel like more of a done deal.

Poppy was his.

He'd spent last night in bed with her working to affirm that.

A pregnancy just made it that much more final.

"I broke up with you last night," she pointed out.

"Yes, you did a very good impression of a woman who was broken up with me. Particularly when you cried out my name during your… Was it your third or fourth orgasm?"

"That has nothing to do with whether or not we should be together. Whether or not we should get married."

"Well, now there's no question about whether or not we're getting married. You're having my baby."

"This is not 1953. That is not a good enough reason to get married."

He frowned. "I disagree."

"I'm not going to just jump into marriage with you."

"You're being unreasonable. You were more than willing to jump into marriage with me when you agreed to my proposal. Now suddenly when we're having a child you can't *jump into* anything? You continually *jump into* my bed, Poppy, so you can't claim we don't have the necessary ingredients to make a marriage work."

"Do you love me?" There was a challenge in her eyes, a stubborn set to her chin.

"I care very much about you," he responded.

It was the truth. The honest truth. She was one of the most important people in his life.

"But you're not in love with me."

"I already told you—"

"Yes. You're not going to do love. Well, you know what? I've decided that it feels fake if we're not in love."

"The fact that you're pregnant with my child indicates it's real enough."

"You don't understand. You don't understand anything."

"You sound like a sixteen-year-old girl having an argument with her parents. You would rather have some idealistic concept that may never actually happen than make a family with me?"

"I would rather… I would rather none of this was happening."

It felt like a slap, and he didn't know why.

That she didn't want him. Didn't seem to want the baby. He couldn't sort out the feeling it gave him. The sharp, stabbing sensation right around the area of his heart.

But he could reason through it. He was right, and her hysterics didn't change that.

There was an order to things. An order of operations, like math. That didn't change based on how people felt.

He understood…nothing right now. Nothing happening inside him, or outside him.

But he knew what was right. And he knew he could count on his brain.

It was the surest thing. The most certain.

So he went with that.

"But it is happening," he said, his voice tight. "You are far too practical to discard something real for some silly fantasy."

Her face drained of color. "So it's a *fantasy* that someone could love me."

"That isn't what I meant. It's a fantasy that you're going to find someone else who can take care of you like I can. Who is also the father of your child. Who can make you come the way that I do."

"Maybe it's just easy for me. You don't know. Neither do I. I've only had the one lover."

That kicked up the fire and heat in his stomach, and he shoved it back down because this was not about what he felt. Not about what his body wanted.

"Trust me," he bit out. "It's never this good."

"I can't do this." She pressed a balled-up fist to her eyes.

"That's too bad," he said. "Because you will."

Resolve strengthened in him like iron. She was upset. But there was only one logical way forward. It was the only thing that made sense. And he was not going to let her take a different route. He just wasn't.

"I don't have to, Isaiah."

"You want your child growing up like you did? Being shuffled between homes?"

She looked like he'd hit her. "Foster care is not the same as sharing custody, and you know that. Don't you dare compare the two. I would have been thrilled to have two involved parents, even if I did have to change houses on the weekends. I didn't have that, and I never have had that. Don't talk about things you don't understand."

"I understand well enough. You're being selfish."

"I'm being *reasonable*!"

Reasonable.

Reasonable to her was them not being together. Reasonable to her was shoving him out of her life now that he'd realized just how essential she was.

"How is it reasonable to deny your child a chance at a family?" he asked. "All of us. Together. At my parents' house for dinners. Aunts and uncles and cousins. How is it unreasonable for me to want to share that with you instead of keeping my life and yours separate?"

"Isaiah…"

He was right, though. And what he wanted wasn't really about what he wanted. It was about logic.

And he wasn't above being heavy-handed to prove that point.

"If you don't marry me, I'm going to pursue full custody of our child," he said, the words landing heavily in the room.

Her head popped up. "You what?"

"And believe me, I'll get it. I have money. I have a family to back me up. I can make this very difficult for you. I don't want to, Poppy. That's not my goal. But I will have my way."

The look on her face, the abject betrayal, almost made him feel something like regret. Almost.

"I thought you were my friend," she said. "I thought you cared about me."

"I do. Which is why I'm prepared to do this. The best thing. The right thing. I'm not going to allow you to hurt our child in the name of friendship. How is that friendship?"

"Caring about someone doesn't just mean running them over until they do what you want. Friendship and caring goes both ways." She pressed her hand to her chest. "What I feel—*what I want*—has to matter."

"I know what you *should* want," he insisted.

If she would only listen. If she could, she'd understand what he was doing. In the end, it would be better if they were together. There was no scenario where their being apart would work, and if he had to play hardball to get her there, he damn well would.

"That isn't how wanting works. It's not how feelings work." She stood up, and she lifted her fist and slammed it down onto his chest. "It's not how any of this works, you robot."

He drew back, shock assaulting him. Poppy was one of the only people who had never looked at him that way before. Poppy had always taken pains to try to understand him.

"I'm a robot because I want to make sure my child has a family?" he asked, keeping his voice low.

"Because you don't care about what I want."

"I *want* you to want what *I* want," he said, holding her fist against his chest where she had hit him. "I want for this to work. How is that not feeling?"

"Because it isn't the *right feeling*."

Those words were like a whip cracking over his insides.

He had *never* had the right feelings. He already knew that. But with Poppy his feelings hadn't ever felt wrong before. *He* hadn't felt wrong before.

She'd been safe. Always.

But not now. Not now he'd started to care.

"I'm sorry," he said, his voice low. "I'm sorry I can't open up my chest and rearrange everything for you. I'm sorry that you agreed to be engaged to me, and then I didn't transform into a different man."

"I never said that's what I wanted."

"It *is* what you wanted. You wanted being with me to look like being with someone else. And you know what? If you weren't pregnant, I might've been able to let you walk away. But it's too late now. This is happening. The wedding is not off."

"The wedding *is* off," she insisted.

"Look at me," he said, his voice low, fierce. "Look at me and tell me if you think I was joking about taking custody."

Her eyes widened, her lips going slack. "I've always cared about you," she said, her voice shaking. "I've always tried to understand you. But I think maybe I was just pretending there was a heart in your chest when there never was."

"You can fling all the insults you want at me. If I'm really heartless, I don't see how you think that's going to make a difference."

Then she let out a frustrated cry and turned and fled the room, leaving him standing there feeling hollowed out.

Wishing that he was exactly what she had accused him of being.

But if he were heartless, then her words—her rejection—wouldn't feel like a knife through his chest.

If he were a robot, he wouldn't care that he couldn't find a way to order his feelings exactly to her liking.

But he did care.

He just had no idea what to do about it.

# Ten

Ultimately, it wasn't Isaiah's threats that had her agreeing to his proposal.

It was what he'd said about family.

She was angry that it had gotten inside her head. That it had wormed its way into her heart.

No. Angry was an understatement.

She was *livid*.

She was also doing exactly what he had asked her to do.

The date for their wedding was now Christmas Eve. Of all the ridiculous things. Though, she supposed that would give her a much stronger association with the holiday than she'd had before.

His family was thrilled.

Poppy was not.

And she was still sleeping in her own room.

After that lapse when she had tried to break things off with him a week earlier, she had decided that she really, *really* needed Isaiah not to touch her for a while.

For his part, he was seething around the house with an intensity that she could feel.

But he hadn't tried to change her mind.

Which was good. Because the fact of the matter was he *would* be able to change her mind. With very little effort.

And besides the tension at home, she was involved in things that made her break out in hives.

Literally.

She had been itchy for three days. The stress of trying to plan a wedding that felt like a death march was starting to get to her.

The fact that she was going wedding-dress shopping with Isaiah's mother and sister was only making matters worse.

And yet, here she was, at Something New, the little bridal boutique in Gold Valley, awaiting the arrival of Nancy and Faith.

The little town was even more heavily decorated for the holidays than Copper Ridge. The red brick buildings were lined with lights, wreaths with crimson bows on every door.

She had opted to drive her own car because she had a feeling she was going to need the distance.

She sighed heavily as she walked into the store, the bell above the door signaling her arrival. A bright, pretty young woman behind the counter perked up.

"Hi," she said. "I'm Celia."

"Hi," Poppy said uncomfortably. "I have an appointment to try on dresses."

"You must be Poppy," she said.

"I am," Poppy said, looking down at her hands. At the ring that shone brightly against her dark skin. "I'm getting married."

"Congratulations," Celia said, as though the inane announcement wasn't that inane at all.

"I'm just waiting for..." The words died on her lips. Her future mother-in-law and sister-in-law. That was who she was waiting for.

Isaiah's family really would be her family. She knew that. It was why she'd said yes to this wedding. And somehow it hadn't fully sunk in yet. She wondered if it ever would.

The door opened a few moments later and Faith and Nancy came in, both grinning widely.

"I'm so excited," Faith said.

Poppy shot her an incredulous look that she hoped Nancy would miss. Faith of all people should not be that excited. She knew Isaiah was only marrying Poppy because of the ad.

Of course, no one knew that Isaiah was also marrying her because she was pregnant.

"So exciting," Poppy echoed, aware that it

sounded hollow and lacking in excitement. She was a great assistant, but she was a lousy actress.

Celia ushered them through endless aisles of dresses and gave them instructions on how to choose preferred styles.

"When you're ready," Celia said, "just turn the dresses out and leave them on the rack. I'll bring them to you in the dressing room."

Poppy wandered through her size, idly touching a few of the dresses, but not committing to anything. Meanwhile, Faith and Nancy were selecting styles left and right.

She saw one that caught her eye. It looked as though it was off the shoulder with long sleeves that came to a point over the top of her hand and loops that would go over her middle finger. It was understated, sedate. Very Grace Kelly, which was right in Poppy's wheelhouse. The heavy, white satin was unadorned, with a deep sheen to it that looked expensive.

She glanced at the price tag. *Incredibly* expensive.

It was somewhat surprising that there was such an upscale shop in the small community of Gold Valley, but then the place had become something of a destination for brides who wanted to make a day of dress shopping, and the cute atmosphere of the little gold rush town, with its good food and unique shops, made for an ideal girls' day out.

"Don't worry about that," Nancy said.

"I can't not worry about it," Poppy said, looking back at the price.

"Isaiah is going to pay for all of it," Nancy said. "And he made sure I was here to reinforce that."

"I know it's silly to be worked up about it," Poppy said. "Considering he signs my paychecks. But the thing is…I don't necessarily want to just take everything from him. I don't want him to think that…"

"That you're marrying him for his money?" Faith asked.

"Kind of," Poppy said.

"He isn't going to think that," Nancy said with authority. "He knows you."

"Yes," Poppy said slowly. "I just…" She looked at them both helplessly. "He's not in love with me," she said. Faith knew, and there was no reason that Poppy's future mother-in-law shouldn't know too. She'd thought she wanted to keep it a secret, but she couldn't bear it anymore, not with the woman she was accepting as family.

"I love him," Poppy said. "I want to make that clear. I love him, and I told him not to let on that this was…a convenient marriage. For my pride. But I can't lie to you." She directed that part to his mother. "I can't lie to you and have you think that I reached him or changed him in a way that I haven't. He still thinks this marriage is the height of practicality. And he's happy to throw money at it like he's happy to throw money at any of his problems. He's not paying for this wedding because he cares what I look like in the wedding dress."

She swallowed hard. "He's paying for it because he thinks that making me his wife is going to somehow magically simplify his life."

Nancy frowned. "You love him."

"I do."

"You've loved him for a long time, haven't you?"

Poppy looked down. She could see Faith shift uncomfortably out of the corner of her eye.

"Yes," Poppy confirmed. "I've loved him ever since I met him. He's a wonderful person. I can see underneath all of the… Isaiah. Or maybe that's not the right way of putting it. I don't even have to see under it. I love who he is. And that…not everybody can see just how wonderful he is. It makes it like a secret. My secret."

"I'm not upset with you," Nancy said, taking hold of the wedding dress Poppy was looking at and turning it outward. "I'm not upset with you at all. You love him, and he came barreling at you with all of the intensity that he has, I imagine, and demanded that you marry him because he decided it was logical, am I right?"

"Very."

"I don't see what woman in your position could have resisted."

If only his mother knew just how little Poppy had resisted. Just how much she wasn't resisting him…

"I should have told him no."

"Does he know that you love him?" Faith asked.

"No," Poppy said.

And she knew she didn't have to tell either of them to keep it a secret. Because they just would.

"Maybe you should tell him," Faith pointed out.

Poppy bit back a smart remark about the fact that Faith was single, and had been for as long as Poppy had known her, and Faith maybe didn't have any clue about dealing with unrequited love.

"Love isn't important to him," Poppy said. "He *likes* me. He thinks that's enough."

Nancy shook her head. "I hope he more than likes you. Otherwise that's going to be a cold marriage bed."

Faith made a squeaking sound. "Mom. Please."

"What? Marriage is long, sweetheart. And sometimes you get distant. Sometimes you get irritated with each other. In those times all you've got is the spark."

Faith slightly receded into one of the dress racks. "Please don't tell me any more about your spark."

"You should be grateful we have it," Nancy said pointedly at her daughter. "It's what I want for you in your marriage, whenever you get married. And it's certainly what I want for Poppy and Isaiah."

Poppy felt her skin flushing. "We're covered there."

"Well, that is a relief."

She wasn't going to tell them about the baby. Not now. She was just going to try on wedding dresses.

Which was what they did.

For the next two hours, Poppy tried on wedding dresses. And it all came down to The One. The long-sleeved beauty with the scary price tag and the perfect train that fanned out behind her like a dream.

Celia found a veil and pinned it into Poppy's dark hair. It was long, extending past the train with a little row of rhinestones along the edge, adding a hint of mist and glitter.

She looked at herself in the mirror, and she found herself completely overwhelmed with emotion.

She was glowing.

There, underneath the lights in the boutique, the white dress contrasted perfectly with her skin tone. She looked like a princess. She felt like one.

And she had…

She looked behind her and saw Nancy and Faith, their eyes full of tears, their hands clasped in front of them.

She had a family who cared about this. Who was here watching her try on dresses.

Who cared for her. For her happiness.

Maybe Isaiah didn't love her, but she loved him. And… His mother and sister loved her. And that offered Poppy more than she had ever imagined she might have.

It was enough. It would be.

Nancy came up behind Poppy and put a hand on Poppy's shoulder. "This is the one. Let him buy it for you. Believe me, he'll cause enough trouble over the course of a lifetime with him that you won't feel bad about spending his money this way."

Poppy laughed, then wiped at a tear that fell down her cheek. "I suppose that's true."

"I'm going to try to keep from hammering advice at you," Nancy said. "But I do have to say this. Love is an amazing thing. It's an inexhaustible resource. I've been married a long time. And over the course of that many decades with someone, there are a lot of stages. Ebbs and flows. But if you keep on giving love, as much as you have, you won't run out. Give it even when it's not flowing to you. Give it when you don't feel like it. If you can do that… That's the best use of love that I can think of. It doesn't mean it's always easy. But it's something you won't regret. Love is a gift. When you have it, choosing to give it is the most powerful thing you can do."

Poppy looked back at her reflection. She was going to be a bride. And more than that, she was going to be Isaiah's wife. He had very clear ideas about what he wanted and didn't want from that relationship. He had very definite thoughts on what he felt and didn't feel.

She had to make a decision about that. About what she was going to let it mean to her.

The problem was, she had spent a lot of years wanting love. Needing love. From parents who were unable to give it for whatever reason. Because they were either too captivated by drugs, or too lost in the struggle of life. She had decided, after that kind of childhood, after the long years of being shuffled between foster homes, that she didn't want to expose herself to that kind of pain again.

Which was exactly what Isaiah was doing.

He was holding himself back. Holding his love back because he'd been hurt before. And somehow... somehow she'd judged that. As if she was different. As if she was well-adjusted and he was wrong.

But that wasn't true.

It was a perfect circle of self-protection. One that was the reason why she had nearly broken the engagement off a week ago. Why she was holding herself back from him now.

And they would never stop.

Not until one of them took a step outside that self-created box.

She could blame her parents. She could blame the handful of foster families who hadn't been able to care for her the way she had needed them to. She could blame the ones who had. The ones she had loved deeply, but whom she had ultimately had to leave, which had caused its own kind of pain.

She could blame the fact that Isaiah had been unavailable to her for all those years. That he had belonged to Rosalind, and somehow that had put him off-limits.

But blame didn't matter. The reasons didn't really matter.

The only thing that mattered was whether or not she was going to change her life.

No one could do it for her.

And if she waited for Isaiah to be the first to take that step, then she would wait forever.

His mother was right. Love was a gift, and you could either hoard it, keep it close to your chest where it wouldn't do a thing for anyone, or you could give it.

Giving her love was the only thing that could possibly open up that door between them. If she wanted him to love her, wanted him to find the faith to love her, she'd have to be the first one to stop protecting herself.

Poppy would have to open up her arms. Stop holding them in front of her, defensive and closed off.

Which was the real problem. Really, it had been all along.

That deeply rooted feeling of unrequited love that she'd had for Isaiah had been incredibly important to her. It had kept her safe. It had kept her from going after anyone else. It had kept her insulated.

But she couldn't continue that now.

Not if she wanted a hope at happiness. Not if she wanted even the smallest chance of a relationship with him.

Someone was going to have to budge first. And she could be bitter about the fact that it had to be her, but there was no point to that.

It was simple.

This wasn't about right or wrong or who should have to give more or less. Who should have to be brave.

She could see that she should.

And if she loved him… Well. She had to care more for him and less for her own comfort.

"I think I might need to give a little bit more love," Poppy said softly.

"If my son doesn't give back to you everything that you deserve, Poppy, you had better believe that I will scar him myself."

"I do believe it," Poppy said.

And if nothing else, what she had learned in that moment was invaluable.

Somebody was in her corner.

And not only had she heard Nancy say it, Poppy believed it. She couldn't remember the last time that had been true.

This was family.

It was so much better than she had ever imagined it could be.

# Eleven

It was late, and Isaiah was working in his home office. His eyes were starting to get gritty, but he wasn't going to his room until he was ready to pass out. It was the only way he could get any sleep at all these days.

Lying in bed knowing she was just down the hall and he couldn't have her was torture. Distance and exhaustion were the only things he could do to combat the restlessness.

He looked up, catching his reflection in the window, along with the reflection of the lamp on his desk.

It was dark out. So dark he couldn't see anything. But he knew the view well. The mountains and hills that were outside that window. A view he had carefully curated after growing tired of the gray landscape of Seattle.

Poppy had been out shopping all day, and he hadn't seen her since she'd left that morning. But he had been thinking about her.

It was strange. The way his feelings for her were affected. A borderline obsession with a woman who should feel commonplace to him in many ways. She had been a part of his office furniture for the past decade.

Except, she'd always been more than that.

Yes. That was true. She always had been.

She was remarkable, smart and funny. Funny in a way he could never really manage to be. More than once, he had wished he could capture that sweetness and hold it to himself just for a little while.

Not that she was saccharine. No. She had no issues taking strips off his hide when it was necessary.

She was also so damn sexy he couldn't think of anything else, and she was starting to drive him insane.

He didn't have any practice with restraint. Over the years, he had been involved mostly in casual hookups, and the great thing about those was they could absolutely happen on his schedule. If the woman didn't matter, then all that was needed was time spent in an appropriate location, and a woman—any woman— would eventually indicate she was available.

But now, he was at the point where not just any woman would do. He needed Poppy.

She was still withholding herself from him, and he supposed he could understand. What with the fact that he had made threats to take her child away if she didn't fall in line. It was entirely possible he wasn't her favorite person at the moment.

That bothered him.

He wasn't very many people's favorite person. But Poppy liked him. At least, she had always seemed to. And now, he had found a very unique way of messing that up.

He'd had a lot of friendships not go the distance. Admittedly, this was quite the most creative way he'd had one dissolve. Proposing, getting that same friend pregnant, and then forcing her to marry him.

Not that he was *forcing* her. Not *really*. He was simply giving her a set of incredibly unpleasant options. And forcing her to choose the one she found the least unpleasant.

He supposed he could take some small measure of comfort in the fact that he wasn't the *least* pleasant option.

But then, that had more to do with the baby than with him.

He sighed heavily.

He'd never felt this way about a woman before. The strange sense of constant urgency. To be with her. To fix things with her. The fact that she was angry with him actively bothered him even when she wasn't in the room displaying that anger.

He could feel it.

He could actually feel someone else's emotion. Stronger than his own.

If he wasn't so fed up, he might marvel at that.

He didn't know what was happening to him.

He was obsessing about the desire. Fixated on it. Because that he understood. Sex, he understood.

This need to tear down all the walls inside him so that he could…

He didn't know.

Be closer to her? Have her feel him, his emotions, so difficult and hard to explain, as keenly as he felt hers?

They'd been friends for ten years. Now they were lovers.

His feelings were like nothing he'd ever felt for a friend or a lover.

The door opened behind him, and he didn't have to turn to see that it was Poppy standing in the doorway. She was wearing her favorite red coat that had a high collar and a tightly belted waist, flaring out at her hips. Her hands were stuffed in her pockets, her eyes cast downward.

"How was your day?"

Her voice was so soft it startled him. He turned. "Good. I wish it were over."

"Still working?"

"Yes. Faith is interested in taking on a couple

more projects. I'm just trying to make sure everything balances out."

"I chose a wedding dress."

He had half expected her to say that she had chosen a burlap sack. Or nothing at all. As a form of
protest.

"I'm glad to hear it," he said, not quite sure what
she wanted him to say. Not quite sure where this
was leading at all.

"I've missed you."

The words landed softly, then seemed to sing
down deep into his heart. "I've seen you every day
for the past week."

"That isn't what I meant." A small crease appeared between her brows as she stared at him. "I'm
not going to say I miss the way we used to be. Because I don't. I like so much of what we have now
better. Except…we don't have it right now. Because
I haven't let you get close to me. I haven't let you
touch me."

She pushed away from the door jamb and walked
slowly toward him. His eyes were drawn downward,
to the wicked, black stilettos on her feet. And to her
bare legs. Which was odd, because she was wearing a coat as if she had been outside in the cold, and
he would have thought she would have something
to cover her skin.

"I've missed you touching me," she said, her voice
growing husky. "I've missed touching you."

She lifted her hands, working the button at the

top of her coat, and then the next, followed by the next. It exposed a V of brown skin, the soft, plump curve of her breasts. And a hint of bright yellow lace.

She made it to the belt, working the fabric through the loop and letting the coat fall open before she undid the button behind it, and the next button, and the next. Until she revealed that she had nothing on beneath the coat but transparent yellow lace. Some sort of top that scooped low around her full breasts and ended above her belly button, showing hints of dark skin through the pattern, the darker shadows of her nipples.

The panties were tiny. They covered almost nothing, and he was pleased with that. She left the heels on, making her legs look impossibly long, shapely and exactly what he wanted wrapped around him.

"What did I do to deserve this?" he asked.

It wasn't a game. Not a leading question. He genuinely wanted to know.

"Nothing," she said. She took a step toward him, lifted the delicate high heel up off the ground and pressed her knee into the empty space on the chair, just beside his thigh.

She gripped the back of the chair, leaning forward. "You haven't done anything at all to deserve this. But I want it. I'm not sure why I shouldn't have it. I think… I think this is a mess." Her tongue darted out, slid over her lips, and he felt the action like a slow lick. "*We* are a mess. We have been. For a long time. Together. Apart. But I'd rather be a mess with you than just a mess who lives in your house and wears your ring. I'd rather be a mess with you inside of me. We're going to get married. I'm having your baby. We're going to have to be a family. And I don't know how to…fix us. I don't know how to repair the broken spaces inside of us. I don't know if it's possible. But nothing is going to be fixed, nothing at all if we're just strangers existing in the same space. If I'm still just your personal assistant when I'm at work."

"What are you going to be when you're at work?"

"Your personal assistant. And your fiancée. And later, your wife. We can't separate these things. Not anymore. We can't separate ourselves."

She pressed her fingertips against his cheek and dragged her hand back, sliding her thumb over his lower lip. "I'm so tired of being lonely. Feeling like… nobody belongs to me. That I don't belong to anyone."

Those words echoed inside him, and they touched something raw. Something painful. He felt… He felt as if they could be words that were coming out of his own mouth. As if she was putting voice to his own pain, a pain he had never before realized was there.

"I want you," she said.

He reached out, bracing his hands on her hips, marveling at the erotic sight of that contrast. His paler hand over the deep rich color of her skin.

A contrast. And still a match.

Deep and sexual and perfect.

He leaned forward and pressed a kiss to her breast, to the bare skin just above the edge of lace. And she gasped, letting her head fall back. It was the most erotic sight. Perfect and indulgent, and something he wanted to hold on to and turn away from with matching intensity.

He wanted her to make him whole. He wanted to find the thing that she was talking about. That depth. That sense of belonging.

Of not being alone.

Of being understood.

He had never even made that a goal. Not even when he'd been with Rosalind. He'd never imagined that a woman might...understand him. He didn't quite understand himself. No one ever had.

He was different. That was all he knew.

He didn't know how to show things the way other people did. Didn't know how to read what was happening right in front of him sometimes.

Was more interested in the black-and-white numbers on a page than the full-color scene in front of him.

He couldn't change it. Didn't know if he would even if he could. His differences were what had made him successful. Made him who he was. But there were very few people willing to put up with that, with him.

But Poppy always had.

She had always been there. She had never— except for the day when she'd hit him in the chest and called him a robot—she had never acted like him being different was even a problem.

Maybe she was the one who could finally reach him. Maybe she was the one he could hold on to.

"I want you," he said, repeating her words back to her.

"I'm here," she said, tilting his face up, her dark eyes luminous and beautiful as she stared down at him. "I'm giving myself to you." She leaned forward, her lips a whisper from his. "Can I be yours, Isaiah?"

"You already are."

He closed the distance between them and claimed her mouth with his.

It was like a storm had exploded. He pulled her onto his lap, wrapping his arms around her tightly as he kissed her. As he lost himself in her. He wanted there to be nothing between them. Not the T-shirt and jeans he was wearing, not even the beautiful lace that barely covered her curves.

*Nothing.*

Nothing but her.

A smile curved his lips. She could maybe keep the shoes. Yes, he would love for her to have those shoes on when he draped her legs over his shoulders and thrust deep inside her.

"I want you so much," he said. The words were torn from him. Coming from somewhere deep and real that he wasn't normally in touch with. "I think I might die if I don't have you."

"I've been in front of you for ten years," she whispered, kissing the spot right next to his mouth, kissing his cheek. "Why now?"

Because he had seen her. Because she had finally kissed him. Because…

"I don't see the world the way everyone else does," he whispered. "I know that. Sometimes it takes an act of God for me to really notice what's happening in front of me. To pull me out of that space in my head. I like it there. Because everything makes sense. And I put people in their place, so I can navigate the day with everything just where I expect it. I can never totally do that with you, Poppy. You always occupied more spaces than you were supposed to.

"I hired you, but you were never only my assistant. You became my friend. And then, you wouldn't stay there either. I put control above everything else. I always have. It's the only way to… For me to make the world work. If I go in knowing exactly what to expect, knowing what everything is. What everyone is. And that's how I didn't see. But then…the minute our lips touched, I knew. I knew, and I can't go back to knowing anything different."

"You like blondes," she pointed out.

"I don't," he responded.

"Rosalind was blonde," Poppy said, brazenly speaking the name she usually avoided at all costs. "And there have been a string of them ever since."

"I told you. I like certainty. Blondes are women I'm attracted to. At least, that was an easy way to think of it. I like to bring order to the world in any way I can."

"And that kept you from looking at me?"

He searched her face, trying to get an idea of what she was thinking. He searched himself, because he didn't know the answer. She was beautiful, and the fact that he hadn't been obsessed with her like this for the past decade was destined to remain a mystery to him.

"Maybe."

She touched his face, sliding her palms back, holding him. "You are not difficult," she said. "Not to me. I like you. All of you."

"No," he responded, shaking his head. "You... You put up with me, I'm sure. And I compensate for the ways that I'm difficult by..."

"No, Isaiah. I like all of you. I always have. There's no putting up with anything."

He hadn't realized how much words like that might mean. Until they poured through him like sunshine dipping down into a low, dark valley. Flooding him with light and warmth.

When he'd been younger, he'd had a kind of boundless certainty in his worldview. But as he'd gotten older—as he'd realized that the way he saw things, the way he perceived interactions and emotions, was often different from the other people involved—he'd started questioning himself.

The older he'd gotten the more he'd realized. How difficult people found it to be his friend. How hard he found it sometimes to carry on a conversation another person wanted to have when he just wanted to charge straight to the point.

How much his brother Joshua carried for him, with his lightning-quick response times and his way with words.

Which had made him wonder how much his parents had modified for him back before he'd realized he needed modification at all.

And with that realization came the worry. About how much of a burden he might be.

But not to Poppy.

He reached up and wrapped his fingers around her slender wrists, holding her hands against his face. He looked at her. Just looked. He didn't have words to respond to what she had said.

He didn't have words.

He had nothing but his desire for her, twisting in his gut, taking him over. Control was the linchpin in his life. It was essential to him. But not now. Now, only Poppy was essential. He wanted her to keep touching him.

Control could wait. It could be set aside for now.

Because letting go so he could hold on to this—to her—was much more important.

It was necessary.

He slid her hands back, draping her arms over his shoulders so she was closer to him, so she was holding on to him. Then he cradled her face, dragging her mouth to his, claiming her, deep and hard and long. Pouring everything that he felt, everything he couldn't say, into this kiss. Into this moment.

He pulled away, sliding his thumb across her lower lip, watching as heat and desire clouded her dark eyes. He could see her surrender to the same need that was roaring through him.

"I always have control," he mumbled, pressing a kiss to her neck, another, and then traveling down to her collarbone. "Always."

He pressed his hand firmly to the small of her back, holding her against him as he stood from the chair, then lowered them both down onto the floor.

He reached behind her and tugged at the top she was wearing. He didn't manage to get hold of the snaps, and he tore the straps, the elastic popping free, the cups falling away from her breasts.

He didn't have to tell her he was out of control. She knew. He could see it. In the heat and fire burning in her dark eyes, and in the subtle curve of her full lips.

She knew that he was out of control, for her. And she liked it.

His efficient, organized Poppy had a wild side. At least, she did with him.

Only for him.

Suddenly, the fact that she had never been with another man before meant everything. This was his.

She was his.

And it mattered.

More than he would have ever thought it could.

He had never given thought to something like that before. He didn't know why he did now. Except... Poppy.

Poppy, who had always been there.

She was a phenomenon. Someone he couldn't understand, someone he wasn't sure he wanted to understand. He didn't mind her staying mysterious. An enigma he got to hold in his arms. As long as this burning bright glory remained.

If he stopped to think, she might disappear. This moment might vanish completely, and he couldn't bear that.

She tore at his clothes too, wrenching them away from his body, making quick work of his shirt before turning her attention to his pants.

As she undressed him, he finished with her clothes, capturing her nipple in his mouth, sucking it in deep. Tasting her. Relishing the feel of her, that velvet skin under his tongue. The taste of her.

It wasn't enough. It never would be. Nothing ever would be.

He felt like his skin was hypersensitized, and that feeling ran all the way beneath his skin, deeper. Making him feel...

Making him *feel*.

He pressed his face into the curve of her neck, kissing her there, licking her. She whimpered and shifted beneath him, wrapping her fingers around his thick length, squeezing him. He let his head fall back, a hoarse groan on his lips.

"Not like that," he rasped. "I need to… No, Poppy. I need you."

"But you have me." She looked innocent. Far too innocent for the moment.

She stroked him, sliding her fingers up and down his length. Then she reached forward, planting her free hand in the center of his chest and pushing him backward slightly. He didn't have to give. He chose to. Because he wanted to see what she would do. He was far too captivated by what might be brewing beneath the surface.

Her breasts were completely bare for him. And then she leaned forward, wrapping her lips around the head of his erection, sliding down slowly as she took all of him into her mouth.

He gritted his teeth, her name a curse on his lips as he grabbed hold of her dark curls and held on tightly while she pleasured him with her mouth. He was transfixed by the sight of her. By the way she moved, unpracticed but earnest. By the way she made him feel.

"Have you ever done this before?" He forced the words out through his constricted throat.

The answer to that question shouldn't matter. It was a question he never should have asked. He'd never cared before, if one of his partners had other lovers. He would have said he preferred a woman with experience.

Not with Poppy. The idea of another man touching her made him insane.

She licked him from base to tip like a lollipop, and then looked up at him. "No."

He swore, letting his head fall back as she took him in deep again.

"Does that matter to you?" she asked, angling her head and licking him.

"Don't stop," he growled.

"Does it matter, Isaiah?" she repeated. "Do you want to be the only man I've ever touched like this? Do you want to know you that you're the only man I've ever seen naked?"

His stomach tightened, impossibly. And he was sure he was going to go right over the edge as her husky, erotic words rolled over him.

"Yes," he bit out.

"Why?"

"Because I want you to be mine," he said, his tone hard. "Only mine."

"I said I was yours," she responded, stoking the length of him with her hand as she spoke. "You're the only man I've ever wanted like this."

His breath hissed out through his teeth. "Me?"

"The only one. From the time you hired me when I was eighteen. I could never... I wanted to date other men. But I just couldn't. I didn't want them. Isaiah, I only wanted you."

Her dark eyes were so earnest as she made the confession, so sincere. That look touched him, all the way down. Even to those places he normally felt were closed off.

She kissed his stomach, up higher to his chest, and then captured his lips again.

"I want you," she said. "Please."

She didn't have to ask twice. He lowered her onto her back and slipped his fingers beneath the waistband of those electric yellow panties, sliding his fingers through her slick folds slowly, slowly, drawing out all that slick wetness, drawing out her pleasure. Until she was whimpering and bucking beneath him. Until she was begging him.

Then he slipped one finger deep inside her, watched as her release found her. As it washed over her like a wave. It was the most beautiful thing he'd ever seen.

But it wasn't enough.

He pulled her panties off and threw them onto the floor, positioning himself between her thighs, pressing himself to the entrance of her body and thrusting in, rough and decisive. Claiming her. Showing her exactly who she belonged to.

Just as he belonged to her.

He lost himself completely, wrapped in her, consumed by her. That familiar scent, vanilla and spice, some perfume Poppy had always worn, mingling with something new. Sweat. Desire. Skin.

What they had been collided with what they were now.

He gripped her hips, thrust into her, deep and hard, relishing her cry of pleasure as he claimed her. Over and over again.

She arched underneath him, crying out his name, her fingernails digging into his skin as her internal muscles pulsed around him.

And he let go. He came on a growl, feral and unrestrained, pleasure like fire over his skin, in his gut.

And when it was over, he could only hold her. He couldn't speak. Couldn't move. Didn't want to.

He looked down at her, and she smiled. Then she pressed her fingers to his lips.

He grabbed her wrist, kissed her palm. "Come to bed with me," he said.

"Okay."

# Twelve

At three in the morning, Isaiah decided that they needed something to eat. Poppy sat on the counter wearing nothing but his T-shirt, watching as he fried eggs and bacon.

She wondered if this was…her life now. She could hardly believe it. And yet, she didn't want to believe anything different.

She ached just looking at this man.

He was so…him. Undeniably. So intense and serious, and yet now, there was something almost boyish about him with his dark hair falling into his eyes, his expression one of concentration as he flipped the eggs in the pan flawlessly without breaking a yolk.

But then, he was shirtless, wearing a pair of low-slung gray sweatpants that seemed perilously close to falling off. His back was broad and muscular, and she enjoyed the play of those muscles while he cooked.

Just that one moment, that one expression on his face, could come close to being called boyish. The rest of him was all man.

He served up the eggs and bacon onto a plate, and he handed Poppy hers, then set his on the counter beside her. He braced himself on the counter, watching her expectantly.

"Do you often have midnight snacks?" she asked.

"No," he said. "But then, tonight isn't exactly routine. Eat."

"Are you trying to fortify me so we can have sex again?"

His lips curved upward. "Undoubtedly."

"This bacon is tainted with ulterior motives," she said, happily taking a bite.

"You seem very sad about that."

"I am." She looked down, then back up, a bubble of happiness blooming in her chest.

"I wanted to make sure you were taken care of," he said, his voice suddenly serious. "Do you feel okay?"

"Yes," she said, confused for a moment.

"No…nausea, or anything like that?"

Right. Because of the baby. So he wasn't only concerned about her. She fought off a small bit of disappointment.

"I feel fine," she said.

"Good," he said.

"Because if I had morning sickness I'd have to miss work?" she asked, not quite certain why she was goading him.

"No. Because if you were sick it would upset me to see you like that."

Suddenly, she felt achingly vulnerable sitting here like this with him.

Isaiah.

She was having his baby. She'd just spent the past couple of hours having wild sex with him. And now she just felt...so acutely aware of who she was. With her hair loose and curly, falling into her face that was free of makeup. Without her structured dresses and killer high heels.

She was just Poppy Sinclair, the same Poppy Sinclair who'd bounced from home to home all through her childhood. Who had never found a family who wanted her forever.

Her throat ached, raw and dry.

His large hand cupped her chin, tilted her face upward. "What's wrong?"

Her heart twisted. That show of caring from him made the vulnerability seem like it might not be so bad. Except...even when he was being nice, it hurt.

She definitely liked a little bit of opposition in her life, and Isaiah was always around to provide that. Either because of her unrequited feelings, or because he was such an obstinate, hardheaded man.

Somehow, all of that was easier than…feeling. It was all part of remaining closed off.

This…opening up was hard, but she had expected that. She hadn't expected it to be painful even when nothing bad was happening.

"I was just thinking," she said.

"About?"

"Nothing specifically," she said.

Just about who she was, and why it was almost ludicrous that she was here now. With him. With so many beautiful things right within her reach.

A family. A husband. A baby.

Passion.

*Love.*

"You can tell me," he said, his gray eyes searching.

"Why do you *want* me to tell you?" she pressed.

"Because you're mine. Anything that is bothering you… Give it to me. I want to…help. Listen."

"Isaiah…" Her eyes burned.

"Did I make you cry?" He looked genuinely concerned by that. He lifted his hand, brushed his thumb beneath the corner of her eye, wiping away a tear she hadn't realized was there.

"You didn't," she said. She swallowed hard. "I was just… It's stupid."

"Nothing is stupid if it makes you cry."

"I was thinking, while I was sitting here watching you take care of me, that I don't remember what it's like to have someone care for me like this. Because…

I'm not sure anyone ever really has. People definitely showed me kindness throughout my life—I'm not saying they didn't. There were so many families and houses. They blur together. I used to remember everyone's names, but now the earlier homes are fading into a blur. Even the people who were kind.

"I remember there was a family… They were going to take me to the fair. And I'd never been before. I was so excited, Isaiah. So excited I could hardly contain myself. We were going to ride a Ferris wheel, and I was going to have cotton candy. I'd never had it before." She took another bite of her bacon and found swallowing difficult.

"The next day, that family found out that the birth mother of a sibling group they were fostering had given birth to another baby. Child services wanted to arrange to have the baby brought in right away. And…that required they move me. The baby had to be with her half siblings. It was right. It made sense."

"You didn't get to go to the fair."

She blinked and shook her head. A tear rolled down her cheek, and she laughed. "It's stupid to still be upset about it. I've been to the fair. I've had cotton candy. But I just… I can remember. How it hurt. How it felt like the world was ending. Worse, I think, is that feeling that nothing in the world is ever stable. That at any moment the rug is going to be pulled out from underneath me. That everything good is just going to vanish. Well, like cotton candy once it hits your tongue."

"I want to take care of you," he said, looking at her, his gray eyes fierce. "Always."

"Don't make promises you can't keep," she said, her stomach churning.

"Don't you trust me?"

She wanted to. But he didn't love her. And if they didn't share love, she wasn't sure what the bond was supposed to be. They had one. She didn't doubt that. And she loved him more than ever.

They would have the baby.

Once they were married it would feel better. It would feel more secure.

"I don't know if you can…understand. But… You've been one of the most constant people I've ever had in my life. Rosalind and I don't see each other very often, but she made sure I was taken care of. She didn't forget me. She's my family. And you… You're my family too."

"If you want to invite Rosalind to the wedding you can," he said.

She blinked. Stunned, because usually any mention of Rosalind's name earned her nothing but stony silence or barely suppressed rage. "She can come to our…wedding?"

"She matters to you," Isaiah said. "And what happened between the two of us isn't important anymore."

"It isn't?" Hope bloomed in her heart, fragile and new, like a tiny bud trying to find its way in early spring. "But she…broke your heart," Poppy finished.

"But now I have you. The rest doesn't matter."

It wasn't the declaration she wanted, but it was something. Better than the promise of a fair or cotton candy or anything like it.

And she wanted to hope.

So she did.

And she leaned forward and kissed him. With each pass of his lips over hers, she let go of a little more of the weight she carried and held on to him a little bit tighter.

# Thirteen

Isaiah had actually taken a lunch break, which wasn't like him, and then it had turned into a rather long lunch. In fact, he had been out of the office for almost two hours, and Poppy couldn't remember the last time he had done that in the middle of the day. She was almost sure he never had, unless he'd taken her with him because it was a working lunch and he had needed somebody to handle the details.

It made her edgy to have him acting out of character.

At least, that's what she told herself. In reality, she just felt a little edgy having him out of her sight. Like he might disappear completely if she couldn't keep tabs on him. Like everything that had happened between them might be imaginary after all.

She tried to relax her face, to keep her concern from showing. Even though there was no one there to see it. It was just… The situation made her feel tense all over. And she shouldn't. Last night had been…

She had never experienced anything like it. Never before, and the only way she would again was if…

*If* they actually got married.

*If* everything actually worked out.

She placed her hand lightly on her stomach and sent up a small prayer. She just didn't want to lose any of this.

She'd never had so much.

She sighed and stood up from her desk. She needed some coffee. Something to clear her head. Something to make her feel less like a crazy lady who needed to keep a visual on her fiancé at all times.

Of course, she *was* a crazy lady who wanted a visual on her fiancé at all times, but, it would be nice if she could pretend otherwise.

Then the door to her office opened and she turned and saw Isaiah standing there in the same black T-shirt and jeans he'd been wearing when he left. But his arm was behind his back, and his expression was…

She didn't think she had ever seen an expression like that on his face before.

"What are you doing?" she asked.

"I went out looking for something for you," he said, his expression serious. "It was harder to find than I thought it would be."

"Because you didn't know what to get me?"

"No. Because it turns out I had no idea where to find what I was looking for."

She frowned. "What's behind your back?"

"Roses would have been easy," he said, and then he moved his hand and she saw a flash of pink. He held out something that was shaped like a bouquet but was absolutely not.

She stood there and just…stared for a moment. Another diamond ring wouldn't have affected her as deeply as this gesture.

Seemingly simple and inexpensive.

To her…it was priceless.

"Cotton candy," she breathed.

"I just wanted to find you some to have with lunch." He frowned. "But now of course it isn't lunchtime anymore."

Isaiah in his most intense state, with his dark brows and heavy beard, holding the pinkest, fluffiest candy in the world, was her new favorite, absurd sight.

She held back a giggle. "Where did you go to get this?"

"There's a family fun center in Tolowa that has it, funnily enough."

"You drove all the way to… Isaiah." She took hold of the cotton candy, then wrenched it from his hand and set it on her desk before wrapping her arms around his neck and kissing him.

"It's going to melt," he said against her lips.

"Cotton candy doesn't melt."

"It shrinks," he pointed out.

"I love cotton candy, don't get me wrong. But I'd rather eat you," she returned.

"I worked hard for that."

She laughed and reached behind her, grabbing hold of the cotton candy and taking a bite, the sugar coating her lips and her tongue. Then she kissed Isaiah again, a sugary, sweet kiss that she hoped expressed some of what she felt.

But not all of it.

Because she hadn't told him.

She was afraid to.

Last night had been a big step of faith, approaching him and giving herself to him like that. It had been her *showing* him what was in her heart. But she knew that wasn't enough. Not really. She needed to say it too.

It had to be said.

She cupped his face and kissed him one more time, examining the lines by his gray eyes, the weathered, rugged look his beard gave him, that sharp, perfect nose and his lips… Lips she was convinced had been made just for her.

Other women had kissed them. She'd seen them do it. But it didn't matter. Because those lips weren't for those women. They were for her. They softened for her. Smiled for her. Only she reached those parts of Isaiah, and she had been the only one for a long time.

And yes, Rosalind had reached something in him Poppy hadn't managed to reach, but if she could do all these other things to him, if she could make him lose control, make him hunt all over creation for cotton candy, then maybe in the future...

It didn't matter. What might happen and what might not. There was only one thing that was certain. And that was how she felt.

She'd loved him for so long. Through so many things. Growing his business, enduring a heartbreak. Long hours, late nights. Fighting. Laughing. Making love.

She'd loved him through all of that.

And she'd love him forever.

Not telling him...worrying about what might happen was just more self-protection, and she was done with that.

"I love you," she said.

He went stiff beneath her touch, but she truly hadn't expected a different reaction. It was going to take him time. She didn't expect a response from him right away; she didn't even want one.

"I've always loved you," she said. "In the beginning, even when you were with Rosalind. And it felt like a horrible betrayal. But I wanted you. And I burned with jealousy. I wanted to have your intensity directed at me. And then when she... The fact that she got to be the only one to ever have it... It's not fair.

"I want it. I love you, Isaiah. I've loved you for ten years, I'll love you for ten more. For all my years. You're everything I could ever want. A fantasy I didn't even know I could create. And I just... I love you. I loved you before we kissed. Before we made love. Before you proposed to me and before I was pregnant. I just...love you."

His expression hadn't changed. It was a wall. Impenetrable and flat. His mouth was set into a grim line, his entire body stiff.

"Poppy..."

"Don't. Don't look at me like you pity me. Like I'm a puppy that you have to kick. I've spent too much of my life being pitied, Isaiah, and I don't want to be pitied by you."

"You have me," he said. "I promise that."

"You don't love me," she said.

"I can't," he said.

She shook her head, pain lancing her heart. "You won't."

"In the end, does it make a difference?"

"In the end, I suppose it doesn't make a difference, but on the journey there, it makes all the difference. *Can't* means there's nothing... Nothing on heaven or earth that could make you change. Won't means you're choosing this. You're choosing to hold on to past hurts, to pain. You're choosing to hold on to another woman instead of holding on to me. You accused me of clinging to a fantasy—of wanting a man who might love me, instead of taking the man who was right in front of me. But what you're doing is worse. You're hanging on to the ghosts of the past rather than hanging on to something real. I think you could love me. I think you might. But you have it buried so far down, underneath all this protection…"

"You don't understand," he said, turning away from her and pushing his fingers through his hair. "You don't understand," he repeated, this time more measured. "It's easy for you. You don't have that disconnect. That time it takes to translate someone's facial expression, what the words beneath their words are, and what it all means. Rosalind was the clumsiest liar, the clumsiest cheat in the entire world, and I didn't know. Because she said she loved me, and so I believed it."

Poppy let out a harsh, wounded breath. "And you don't believe me?"

"I didn't say that."

"But that's what it is. You don't trust me. If you trusted me, then this wouldn't be an issue."

"No," he said. "That isn't true. I felt like a tool when everything happened with Rosalind. She broke places in me I hadn't realized were there to be broken. I don't think you can possibly understand what it's like to be blindsided like that."

Her vision went fuzzy around the edges, her heart pounding so hard she thought she might faint.

"You don't… I just told you one small piece of

what it was like to grow up like I did. How antici-pating what might happen tomorrow was dangerous because you might be in a whole new house with a bunch of strangers the next day. My life was never in my control. Ever. It was dangerous to be comfort-able, dangerous to care. There was a system, there were reasons, but when I was a child all I knew was that I was being uprooted. Again and again."

"I'm sorry. I didn't mean..."

"We've all been hurt. No one gives us a choice about that. But what are you going to do about it? What is the problem? Say it out loud. Tell me. So that you have to hear for yourself how ridiculous this all is."

"It changed something in me," he said. "And I can't... I can't change it back."

"You *won't*. You're a coward, Isaiah Grayson. You're running. From what you feel. From what you *could* feel. You talk about these things you can't do, these things you can't feel. These things you can't understand. But you understand things other people never will. The way you see numbers, the way you fit it all together—that's a miracle. And if your brain worked like everyone else's, then you wouldn't be that person. You wouldn't be the man I love. I don't want you to change who you are. Don't you under-stand that? That's not what I'm asking for. I'm ask-ing for you to hold on to me instead of her."

He took a step back, shaking his head slowly. "Poppy..."

"Where's my big, scary, decisive boss? My stubborn friend who doesn't back down? Or is this request terrifying because I'm asking for something that's not in your head? Something that's in your heart?"

Her own heart was breaking, splintering into a thousand pieces and falling apart inside her chest. She thought she might die from this.

She hadn't expected him to be able to give her a response today, but she hadn't known he was going to launch into an outright denial of his ability to ever, ever love her.

"Maybe I don't have a heart," he said, his voice hard. "Maybe I'm a robot, like you said."

"I don't think that's true. And I shouldn't have said that in the first place."

"But maybe you were closer to the truth than you want to believe. Maybe you don't love me like I am, Poppy. Maybe you just see things in me that aren't there, and you love those. But they aren't real."

She shook her head, fighting back tears. "I don't think that's true. I've been with you for a decade, Isaiah." She looked at his face, that wonderful, familiar face. That man who was destroying everything they'd found.

She wanted to hit him, rage at him. "I *know you*. I know you care. I've watched you with your family. I've watched you work hard to build this business with Joshua and Faith, to take it to the next level with the merger. You work so hard, and that's not…

empty. Everything you've done to support Faith in her dream of being an architect…"

"It's her talent. I can't take the credit."

"Without you, the money wouldn't flow and that would be the end of it. You're the main artery, and you give it everything. You might not express how you care the way other people do, but you express it in a real, tangible way." He didn't move. Didn't change his expression. "You can love, Isaiah. And other people love you."

He said nothing. Not for a long moment.

"I would never take our child from you," he said finally.

"What?"

"I won't take our child from you. Forcing you to marry me was a mistake. This is a mistake, Poppy."

She felt like that little girl who had been promised a carnival, only to wake up in the morning and have her bags packed again.

The disappointment even came complete with cotton candy.

"You don't want to marry me?"

"I was forcing it," he said. "Because in my mind I had decided that was best, and so because I decided it, it had to be true. But… It's not right. I won't do that to you."

"How dare you? How dare you dump me and try to act like it's for my own good? After I tell you that I love you? Forcing me to marry you was bad enough, but at least then you were acting out of complete emotional ignorance."

"I'm always acting out of emotional ignorance," he said. "Don't say you accept all of me and then act surprised by that."

"Yeah, but sometimes you're just full of shit, Isaiah. And you hide behind those walls. You hide behind that brain. You try to outwit and outreason everything, but life is not a chess game. It's not math. None of this is. Your actions least of all. Because if you added up everything you've said and done over the past few weeks, you would know that the answer equaled love. You would know that the answer is that we should be together. You would know that you finally have what you want and *you're giving it away*.

"So don't try to tell me you're being logical. Don't try to talk to me like I'm a hysterical female asking something ridiculous of you. You're the one who's scared. You're the one who's hysterical. You can stand there with a blank look on your face and pretend that somehow makes you rational, but you aren't. You can try to lie to me. You can try to lie to yourself. But I don't believe it. I refuse."

She took a deep breath. "And I quit. I really do quit this time. I'm not going to be here for your convenience. I'm not going to be here to keep your life running smoothly, to give you what you want when you want it while I don't get my needs met in return. If you want to let me go, then you have to let me go."

She picked up the cotton candy. "But I'm taking

this." She picked up her coat also, and started to walk past him and out of the room. Then she stopped. "I'll be in touch with you about the baby. And I will pay you back for the wedding dress if I can't return it. Please tell… Please tell your mom that I'm sorry. No. Tell them you're sorry. Tell them you're sorry that you let a woman who could never really love you ruin your chance with one who already does."

And then she walked out of the office, down the hall, past Joshua's open door and his questioning expression, through the lobby area, where Faith was sitting curled up in a chair staring down at a computer.

"Goodbye," Poppy said, her voice small and pained.

"What's going on?" Faith asked.

"I quit," Poppy said. "And the wedding is off. And… I think my heart is breaking. But I don't know what else to do."

Poppy found herself standing outside the door, waiting for a whole new life to start.

And, like so many times before, she wasn't confident that there would be anything good in that new life.

She took a breath. No. There would be something good. This time, there was the certainty of that.

She was going to be a mother.

Strangely, out of all this heartbreak, all this brokenness, came a chance at a kind of redemption she had never really let herself believe in.

She was going to be a mother.

It would be her only real chance at having a good mother-daughter relationship. And yes, she would be on the other side of it. But she would give her child the best of herself.

A sad smile touched her lips. Even without meaning to, Isaiah had given her a chance at love. It just hadn't been the kind of love she'd been hoping for.

But…it was still a gift.

And she was going to cling to it with everything she had.

# Fourteen

Isaiah wasn't a man given to excessive drinking, but tonight he was considering it.

By the time he had gotten home from work, Poppy had cleared out her things. He supposed he should have gone after her. Should have left early. But he had been...

He had been frozen.

He had gone through the motions all day, trying to process what had happened.

One thing kept echoing in his head, and it wasn't that she loved him, though that had wrapped itself around his heart and was currently battering at him, making him feel as though his insides had been kicked with a steel-toed boot.

Or maybe just a stiletto.

No, the thing that kept going through his mind was what she'd said about his excuses.

He had known even as he said it out loud that he didn't really believe all the things he'd said. It wasn't true that he couldn't love her.

She had asked if he didn't trust her. And that wasn't the problem either.

He didn't trust himself.

Emotion was like a foreign language to him. One he had to put in effort to learn so he could understand the people around him. His childhood had been a minefield of navigating friendships he could never quite make gel, and high school and college had been a lot of him trying to date and inadvertently breaking hearts when he missed connections that others saw.

It was never that he didn't feel. It was just that his feelings were in another language.

And he often didn't know how to bridge the gap.

And the intensity of what he felt now was so sharp, so intense that his natural inclination was to deny it completely. To shut it down. To shut it off. It was what he often did. When he thought of those parts of himself he couldn't reach...

He chose to make them unreachable.

It was easier to navigate those difficult situations with others if he wasn't also dealing with his own feelings. And so he'd learned. Push it down. Rationalize the situation.

Emotion was something he could feel, hear, taste

and smell. Something that overtook him completely. Something that became so raw and intense he wanted to cut it off completely.

But with her… He couldn't.

When he was making love with her, at least there was a place for all those feelings to go. A way for them to be expressed. There was something he could do with them. With that roaring in his blood, that sharp slice to his senses.

How could he give that to someone else? How could he… How could he trust himself to treat those emotions the way that they needed to be treated?

He really wanted a drink. But honestly, the explosion of alcohol with his tenuous control was likely a bad idea. Still, he was considering it.

There was a heavy knock on his front door and Isaiah frowned, going down the stairs toward the entry.

Maybe it was Poppy.

He jerked the door open and was met by his brother Joshua.

"What are you doing here?" Isaiah asked.

"I talked to Faith." Joshua shoved his hands in his pockets. "She said Poppy quit."

"Yes," Isaiah said. He turned away from his brother and walked toward the kitchen. He was going to need that drink.

"What did you do?"

"You assume I did something?" he asked.

Isaiah's anger rang a little bit hollow, considering he knew that it was his fault. Joshua just stared at him.

Bastard.

Was he so predictably destructive in his interpersonal relationships?

Yes.

He knew the answer to that without thinking.

"I released her from her obligation," Isaiah said. "She was the one who chose to leave."

"You released her from her obligation? What the hell does that mean?"

"It means I was forcing her to marry me, and then I decided not to." He sounded ridiculous. Which in and of itself was ridiculous, since *he* never was.

His brother pinched the bridge of his nose. "Start at the beginning."

"She's pregnant," Isaiah said.

Joshua froze. "She's…"

"She's pregnant," Isaiah repeated.

"How…"

"You know exactly how."

"I thought the two of you had an arrangement. Meaning I figured you weren't going to go…losing control," Joshua said.

"We had something like an arrangement. But it turned out we were very compatible. Physically."

"Yes," Joshua said, "I understood what you meant by compatible."

"Well, how was I supposed to know? You were just standing there staring at me." He rubbed his hand over his face. "We were engaged, she tried to break it off. Then she found out she was pregnant. I told her she had to marry me or I would pursue full custody—"

"Every woman's fantasy proposal. I hope you filmed it so you'll always have a memory of that special moment."

Isaiah ignored his brother. "It was practical. But then…then she wanted things I couldn't give, and I realized that maybe forcing a woman to marry me wasn't the best idea."

"And she's in love with you."

Isaiah sighed heavily. "Yes."

"And you said you couldn't love her back so she left?"

"No," he said. "I said I couldn't love her and I told her I wouldn't force her to marry me. And then she left."

"You're the one who rejected her," Joshua said.

"I don't know how to do this," Isaiah said, his voice rough. "I don't know how to give her what she wants while…while making sure I don't…"

He didn't want to say it because it sounded weak, and he'd never considered himself weak. But he was afraid of being hurt, and if that wasn't weakness, he didn't know what was.

"You can't," Joshua said simply, reading his mind. "Loving someone means loving them at the expense of your own emotional safety. Sorry. There's not another alternative."

"I can't do that."

"Because one woman hurt you?"

"You don't understand," Isaiah said. "It has nothing to do with being hurt once. Rosalind didn't just hurt me, she made a fool out of me. She highlighted every single thing that I've struggled with all my life and showed me how inadequate I am. Not with words. She doesn't even know what she did."

He took a deep breath and continued, "Connecting with people has always been hard for me. Not you, not the family. You all…know how to talk to me. Know how to deal with me. But other people? It's not easy, Joshua. But with her I thought I finally had something. I let my guard down, and I quit worrying. I quit worrying about whether or not I understood everything and just…was with someone for a while. But what I thought was happening wasn't the truth. Everything that should've been obvious was right in front of me."

"But that's not your relationship with Poppy. And it isn't going to be. She's not going to change into something else just because you admit that you're in love with her."

"Poppy is different," Isaiah said. "Whatever I thought I felt then, this is different."

"You love her. And if you don't admit that, Isaiah? Maybe you won't feel it quite so keenly, but you won't have her. You're going to…live in a separate place from the woman you love?"

"I won't be a good father anyway," Isaiah said.

"Why do you think that?"

"How am I going to be a good father when I can't… What am I going to teach a kid about relationships and people? I'm not wired like everyone else."

"And maybe your child won't be either. Or maybe my child will be different, and he'll need his uncle's help. Any of our children could need someone there with him who understands. You're not alone. You're not the only person who feels the way that you do."

Isaiah had never thought about that. About the fact that his own experiences might be valuable to someone else.

"But Poppy…"

"Knows you and loves you. She doesn't want you to be someone else."

Isaiah cleared his throat. "I accused her of that."

"Because she demanded you pull your head out of your ass and admit that you love her?"

"Yes," he admitted.

"Being alone is the refuge of cowards, Isaiah, and you're a lot of things, but I never thought you were a coward. I understand trying to avoid being hurt again. After everything I went through with my ex, I didn't want anything to do with a wife or another baby. But now I have Danielle. I have both a wife and a son. And I'm glad I didn't let grief be the deciding factor in my life. Because, let me tell you something, that's easy. It's easy to let the hard things ruin you.

It's a hell of a lot braver to decide they don't get to control you."

"It hurts to breathe," Isaiah said, his voice rough. "When I look at her."

"If you aren't with her, it'll still hurt to breathe. She just won't be beside you."

"I didn't want a wife so I could be in love," Isaiah said. "I wanted one to make my life easier."

"You don't add another person to your life to make it easier. Other people only make things harder, and you should have a better understanding of that than most. You accept another person into your life because you can't live without them. Because easy isn't the most important thing anymore. She is. That's love. And it's bigger than fear. It has to be, because love itself is so damned scary."

"Why does anyone do it?" Isaiah asked.

"You do it when you don't have a choice anymore. I almost let Danielle walk away from me. I almost ruined the best thing I'd ever been given because of fear. And you tell me why a smart man would do that? Why does fear get to be the biggest emotion? Why can't love win?"

Isaiah stood there, feeling like something had shifted under his feet.

He couldn't outrun emotion. Even when he suppressed it, there was an emotion that was winning: fear.

He'd never realized that, never understood it, until now.

"Think about it," Joshua said.

Then he turned and walked out of the house, leaving Isaiah alone with his obviously flawed thinking.

He loved Poppy.

To his bones. To his soul.

He couldn't breathe for the pain of it, and he had no idea what the hell he was supposed to do with the damned fear that gnawed at his gut.

This had all started with an ad for a wife. With the most dispassionate idea any man had ever hatched.

Him, divorcing himself from feeling and figuring out a way to make his life look like he wanted it to look. To make it look like his parents' lives. His idea of home.

Only now he realized he'd left out the most important thing.

Love.

It was strange how his idea of what he wanted his life to be had changed. He had wanted to get married. He had wanted a wife. And he'd found a way to secure that.

But now he just wanted *Poppy*.

Whether they were married or not, whether or not they had perfect, domestic bliss and Sunday dinners just like his parents, whether they were in a little farmhouse or his monstrosity of a place… It didn't matter. If she was there.

Wherever Poppy was…that was his home.

And if he didn't have her, he would never have a home.

He could get that drink now. Stop the pain in his chest from spreading further, dull the impending realization of what he'd done. To himself. To his life. But he had to feel it. He had to.

He braced himself against the wall and lowered his head, pain starting in his stomach, twisting and turning its way up into his chest. Like a shard of glass had been wedged into the center of his ribs and was pushed in deeper with each breath.

He'd never lost love before.

He'd had wounded pride. Damaged trust.

But he'd never had a broken heart.

Until now.

And he'd done it to himself.

Poppy had offered him all he needed in the world, and he'd been too afraid to take it.

Poppy had lived a whole life filled with heartbreak. With being let down. He'd promised to take care of her, and then he hadn't. He was just another person who'd let her down. Another person who hadn't loved her like she should have been loved.

He should have loved her more than he loved himself.

He clenched his hand into a fist. He was done with this. With this self-protection. He didn't want it anymore.

He wanted Poppy.

Now. Always.

More than safety. More than breathing.

But he'd broken her trust. She'd already loved and

lost so many people in her life, had been let down by parades of people who should have done better, and there was no logical reason for her to forgive him.

He just had to hope that love would be stronger than fear.

# Fifteen

Poppy was a study in misery.

She had taken all her easily moved things and gone back to her house.

She wasn't going to flee the town. She loved her house, and she didn't really have anywhere else to go at the moment. No, she was going to have to sort that out, but later.

She wasn't entirely sure what she wanted. Where she would go.

She would have to find another job.

She could, she knew that. She had amply marketable skills. It was just that… It would mean well and truly closing the door on the Isaiah chapter of her life. Possibly the longest chapter she even had.

So many people had cycled in and out of her life. There had been a few constants, and the Graysons had been some of her most cherished friends. It hurt. Losing him like this. Losing them. But this was just how life went for her. And there was nothing she could do about it. She was always, forever at the mercy of people who simply couldn't...

She swallowed hard.

There was no real furniture left in her house after she'd moved to Isaiah's ranch. She had gathered a duffel bag full of clothes and a sleeping bag. She curled up in the sleeping bag on the floor in the corner of her bedroom and grabbed her cell phone.

There was one person she really owed a phone call.

She dialed her foster sister's number and waited.

"Hello?"

"I hope it's not too late," Poppy said, rolling to her side and looking out the window at the inky black sky.

It had the audacity to look normal out there. Clear and crisp like it was just a typical December night and not a night where her world had crashed down around her.

"Of course not. Jason and I were just getting ready to go out. But that can wait. What's going on?"

"Oh. Nothing... Everything."

"What's going on?" Rosalind repeated, her voice getting serious. "You haven't called in a couple of months."

"Neither have you," Poppy pointed out.

"I know. I'm sorry. I've never been very good at keeping in touch. But that doesn't mean I don't like hearing from you."

"I'm pregnant," Poppy blurted out.

The pause on the other end was telling. But when Rosalind finally did speak, her voice was shot through with excitement. "Poppy, congratulations. I'm so happy for you."

"I'm single," she said as a follow-up.

"Well, I figured you would have altered your announcement slightly if you weren't."

"I don't know what I'm going to do." She pulled her knees up and tucked her head down, holding her misery to her chest.

"If you need money or a place to stay… You know you can always come and stay with me and Jason."

Poppy did know that. Maybe that was even why she had called Rosalind. Because knowing that she had a place with her foster sister made her feel slightly less rootless.

She wouldn't need to use it. At least, she *shouldn't* need to use it. But knowing that Rosalind was there for her helped.

Right now, with the only other anchor in her life removed and casting her mostly adrift, Rosalind was more important than ever.

"Isaiah isn't being a terror about it, is he?" Rosalind asked.

"Not... Not the way you mean," Poppy said slowly. "It's Isaiah's baby."

The silence stretched even longer this time. *"Isaiah?"*

"Yes," Poppy said. "And I know... I know that's... I'm sorry."

"Why are you apologizing to me?" Rosalind sounded genuinely mystified.

"Because he's your...your ex. And I know I don't have a lot of experience with family, but you're the closest thing I have to a sister, and I know you don't...go dating your sister's ex-boyfriends."

"Well. Yes. I suppose so. But he's my *ex*. From a long time ago. And I'm with someone else now. I've moved on. Obviously, so has he. Why would you keep yourself from something you want just because...just because it's something other people might not think was okay? If you love him..."

Poppy realized that the guilt she felt was related to the fact that her feelings for Isaiah had most definitely originated when Isaiah had not been Rosalind's ex.

"I've had feelings for him for a long time," Poppy said quietly. "A really long time."

"Don't tell me you feel bad about that, Poppy," Rosalind said.

"I do," Poppy said. "He was your boyfriend. And you got me a job with him. In that whole time..."

"You didn't *do* anything. It's not like you went after him when were together."

"No."

"I'm the cheater in that relationship." Rosalind sighed heavily. "I didn't handle things right with Isaiah back then. I cheated on him, and I shouldn't have. I should have been strong enough to break things off with him without being unfaithful. But I wasn't."

They'd never talked about this before. The subject of Isaiah had always been too difficult for Poppy. She'd been so angry that Rosalind had hurt him, and then so resentful that her betrayal had claimed such a huge part of his heart.

But Poppy had never really considered…how Rosalind's past might have informed what she'd done.

And considering happiness had made Poppy act a lot like a feral cat, she should have.

"He was the first person who treated me really well, and I felt guilty about it," Rosalind continued. "But gratitude isn't love. And what I felt for him was gratitude. When I met Jason, my whole world kind of turned over, and what I felt for him was something else. Something I had never experienced before.

"I caused a lot of trouble for Isaiah, and I feel bad about it. But you certainly shouldn't feel guilty over having feelings for him. You should… You should be with him. He's a great guy, Poppy. I mean, not for me. He's too serious and just…not *right* for me. But you've known him in a serious way even longer than I have, and if you think he's the guy for you…"

"We were engaged," Poppy said. "But he broke it off."

*"What?"*

"It's a long story." Poppy laughed. "A very Isaiah story, really. We got engaged. Then we slept together. Then I broke up with him. Then I got pregnant. Then we slept together again. Then we kind of…got back engaged… But then he…broke up with me because I told him I was in love with him."

"We really need to not have so much time between phone calls," Rosalind said. "Okay. So… You being in love with him…scared him?"

"Yes," Poppy said slowly.

She wasn't going to bring up Rosalind's part in the issues between Poppy and Isaiah. Mostly because Poppy didn't actually believe they were a significant part. Not specifically. The issues that Isaiah had with love and feelings were definitely on him.

"And you're just going to…let him walk away from what you have?"

"There's nothing I can do to stop him. He said he doesn't love me. He said he doesn't… He doesn't want a relationship like that. There's nothing I can do to change how he feels."

"What did you do when he said that?"

"I yelled at him. And then…I left."

"If I was in love with a guy, I would camp out on his doorstep. I would make him miserable."

"I have some pride, Rosalind."

"I don't," Rosalind said. "I'm a crazy bitch when it comes to love. I mean, I blew up a really good thing to chase after Jason."

"This is… It's different."

"But you love him."

"How many times can I be expected to care for someone and lose them? You know. Better than anyone, you understand what growing up was like for me. For us. People were always just…shuffling us around on a whim. And I just… I can't handle it. Not anymore."

"There's a really big difference between now and then," Rosalind pointed out. "We are not kids. This is what I realized, though a little bit late with Isaiah. I wasn't a child. I didn't have to go along. I had a choice. Child services and foster families and toxic parents don't get to run our lives anymore, Poppy. We are in charge now. You're your own caseworker. You are the one who gets to decide what kind of life you want to have. Who you want to live with. What you'll settle for and what you won't. You don't have to wait for someone to rescue you or accept it when someone says they can't be with you."

"I kind of do. He said…"

"What's the worst that could happen if you fight for him one more time? Just one more?"

Poppy huffed out a laugh. "I'll die of humiliation."

"You won't," Rosalind said. "I guarantee you, humiliation isn't fatal. If humiliation were fatal, I would have died twice before Jason and I actually got married. At *least*. I was insecure and clingy, and a lot of it was because of how our relationship started, which was my own fault. My fear of getting him dirty and losing him dirty, that kind of thing. But…now we've been married for five years, and…none of that matters. Now all that matters is that we love each other. That we have each other. Everything else is just a story we tell and laugh about."

"You know Isaiah. He was very certain."

"I don't actually know Isaiah as well as you do. But you're going to have a baby with him. And… Whether or not you get him in the end, don't you think what you want is worth fighting for? Not for the sake of the baby, or anything like that. But for you. Have you ever fought for *you* before, Poppy?"

She had started to. When Isaiah had broken things off. But…

She didn't know if she really had.

Maybe Rosalind was right. Maybe she needed to face this head-on. Again.

Because nobody controlled the show but her. Nobody told her when to be done except for her.

And pride shouldn't have the last word.

"I love you," Poppy said. "I hope you *know* that. I know we're different. But you've been family to me. And… You're responsible for some of the best things I have in life."

"Well, I'm going to feel guilty if Isaiah breaks your heart."

"Even if he does… I'll be glad he was in my life for as long as he was. I love him. And…being able to love someone like this is a gift. One I don't think I fully appreciated. With our background, just being able to admit my love without fear, without holding back… That's something. It's special. It's kind of a miracle."

"It really is," Rosalind said. "I had a rocky road to Jason. I had a rocky road to love, but Poppy, it's so worth it in the end. I promise you."

"I just hope Isaiah realizes how special it is. How amazing it is. His parents always loved him. He grew up in one house. He…doesn't know that not everyone has someone to love them."

"He might have had all of that, Poppy, but he's never had you. Don't sell yourself short."

Poppy tried to breathe around the emotion swelling in her chest. "If it all works out, you're invited to the wedding," Poppy said decisively.

"Are you sure?"

"Of course. You're my family. And the family I've created is the most important thing I have."

"Good," Rosalind said. "Then go fight for the rest of it."

Poppy would do that. She absolutely would.


Isaiah didn't know for sure that he would find Poppy at her house. He could only hope that he would.

If not, he would have to launch a search of the entire town, which everyone was going to find unpleasant. Because he would be getting in faces and asking for access to confidential records. And while he was confident that ultimately he would get his way, he would rather not cut a swath of rage and destruction through the community that he tried to do business in.

But, desperate times.

He felt like he was made entirely of feelings. His skin hurt from it. His heart felt bruised. And he needed to... He needed to find Poppy and tell her.

He needed to find her and he needed to fix this.

It was 6:00 a.m., and he had two cups of coffee in his hand when he pounded on the door of her house with the toe of his boot.

It took a couple of minutes, but the door finally opened and revealed Poppy, who was standing there in baggy pajama pants with polar bears on them, and a plain shirt. Her hair was exceptionally large and sticking out at all angles, one curl hanging in her face. And she looked...

Not altogether very happy to see him.

"What are you doing here?"

"I brought you coffee."

"Yesterday you brought me cotton candy, and you were still a dick. So explain to me why I should be compelled by the coffee." She crossed her arms and treated him to a hard glare.

"I need to talk to you."

"Well, that works, because I need to talk to you too. Though, I was not going to talk to you at six in the morning."

"Were you asleep?"

"Obviously. It's six in the morning." Then her

shoulders slumped and she sighed, backing away from the door. "No. I wasn't sleeping."

He found himself relieved by that.

"I couldn't sleep at all," she continued. "Because I kept thinking about you. You asshole."

He found that extraordinarily cheering.

"I couldn't sleep either," he said.

"Well, of course not. You lost your assistant. And you had to get your own coffee as a result. Life is truly caving in around you, Isaiah."

"That isn't why I couldn't sleep," he said. "I talked to my brother last night."

"Which one?"

"Joshua. Who was not terribly impressed with me, I have to say."

"Well, I'm not sure who could be terribly impressed with you right at the moment."

She wasn't letting him off easy. And that was all right. He didn't need it to be easy. He just needed to fix it.

"I do feel," he said, his voice coming out so rough it was like a stranger's. "I feel a lot. All the time. It's just easier when I don't. So I'm very good at pushing down my emotions. And I'm very good at separating feelings from a moment. That way I have time to analyze what I feel later, instead of being reactionary."

"Because being reactionary is bad?"

"Yes. Especially when... When I might have read a situation wrong. And I do that a lot, Poppy. I'm a perfectionist. I don't like being wrong."

"This is not news to me," she said.

"I know. You've also known me long enough that you seem to know how to read me. And I... I'm pretty good at reading you too. But sometimes I don't get it right. Feelings are different for me. But it doesn't mean I don't have them. It does mean that sometimes I'm wrong about what's happening. And... I hate that. I hate it more than anything. I hate feeling like everything is okay and finding out it isn't. I hate feeling like something is wrong only to find out that it's not."

"You know everyone makes those mistakes," she said gently. "Nobody gets it completely right all the time."

"I do know that," he said. "But I get it wrong more often than most. I've always struggled with that. I've found ways to make it easier. I use organization. My interest in numbers. Having an assistant who helps me with the things I'm not so great at. All of those things have made it easier for me to have a life that functions simply. They've made it so I don't have to risk myself. So I don't have to be hurt.

"But I'm finding that they have not enabled me to have a full life. Poppy, I don't just want easy. That was a mistake I made when I asked you to find me a wife. I thought I wanted a wife so I could feel the sense of completeness in my personal life that I did my professional life. But what I didn't realize was that things felt complete in my professional life because I was with you every day."

He took a step toward her, wanting to touch her. With everything he had.

"I had you in that perfect space I created for you. And I got to be with you all the time," he continued. "Yours was one of the first faces I saw every morning. And you were always one of the last people I saw before I went home. There was a rightness to that. And I attributed it to…the fact that you were efficient. The fact that you were organized. The fact that I liked you. But it was more than that. And it always has been. It isn't that I didn't think of you when I decided to put an ad in the paper for a wife. You were actually the reason I did it. It's just that… I'm an idiot."

He paused and watched her expression.

"Are you waiting for me to argue with you?" She blinked. "I'm not going to."

"I'm not waiting for you to argue. I just want you to… I want you to see that I mean this. I want you to understand that I didn't do it on purpose. There's just so many layers of protection inside me, and it takes me days sometimes to sort out what's happening in my own chest.

"You are right. I hated it because it wasn't in my head. I hated it because it all comes from that part of me that I find difficult. The part that I feel holds me back. It is amazing to have a brother like Joshua. Someone who's a PR expert. Who seems to navigate rooms and facial expressions and changes in mood seamlessly. I've had you by my side for that. To say the right thing in a meeting when I didn't. To give me your rundown on how something actually went so that I didn't have to."

"I already told you it's not hard for me to do that for you. The way you are doesn't bother me. It's just you. It's not like there's this separate piece of you that has these challenges and then there's you. It's all you. And I could never separate it out. I wouldn't even want to. Isaiah, you're perfect the way you are. Whether there is a label for this or not. Whether it's a disorder or it isn't. It doesn't matter to me. It's all you."

"I bet you resented it a little bit yesterday."

"You hurt me. You hurt me really badly. But I still think you're the best man I know. I still… Isaiah, I love you. You saying terrible things to me one day is not going to undo ten years of loving you."

The relief washing through him felt unlike anything he'd ever experienced before. He wanted to drop to his knees. He wanted to kiss her. Hold her. He wanted to unlock himself and let everything he felt pour out.

Why wasn't he doing that? Why was he standing there stiff as a board when that wasn't at all what he felt?

So he did.

He dropped down to his knees and he wrapped his arms around her, pressing his face against her stomach. Against Poppy and the life that was growing inside her.

"I love you," he whispered. "Poppy, I love you."

He looked up at her, and she was staring down at him, bewildered, as he continued, "I just… I was so afraid to let myself feel it. To let myself want this. To let myself have it. I can't help but see myself as an emotional burden. When I think of everything you do for me… I think of you having to do that in our lives, and it doesn't feel fair. It feels like you deserve someone easier. Someone better. Someone you don't have to act as a translator for."

"I've had a long time to fall in love with other men, Isaiah. But you are the one I love. You. And I already told you that I don't see you and then the way you process emotion. It's all you. The man I love. All your traits, they can't be separated. I don't want them to be. You're not my project. You… You have no idea what you give to me. Because I've never told you. I talked with Rosalind last night."

"You did?"

"Yes." Poppy crouched down, so that they were eye to eye. "She told me I needed to fight for you. That we are not foster children anymore, and I can't live like someone else is in control of my destiny. And she's right. Whether or not you showed up at my house this morning, we were going to talk. Because I was going to come find you. And I was going to tell you again that I love you."

"I'm a lot of work," he said, his voice getting rough.

"I don't care. It's my privilege to have the freedom to work at it. No one is going to come and take me away and move me to a different place. No one is controlling what I do but me. If I choose to work at this, if I choose to love you, then that's my choice.

"And it's worth it. You mean everything to me. You hired me when I was an eighteen-year-old girl who had no job experience, who had barely been in one place for a year at a time. You introduced me to your family, and watching them showed me how love can function in those kinds of relationships. Your family showed me the way people can treat each other. The way you can fight and still care. The way you can make mistakes and still love."

"That's my family. It isn't me."

"I haven't gotten to you yet." She grabbed hold of his chin, her brown eyes steady on his. "You've told me how difficult it is for you to navigate people. But you still do it. You are so loyal to the people in your life. Including me.

"I watched the way you cared for Rosalind. Part of that was hiring me, simply because it meant something to her. Part of that was caring for her, and yes, in the end you felt like you made a mistake, like she made a fool out of you, but you showed that you had the capacity to care deeply.

"You have been the most constant steady presence in my life for the past decade. You've shown me what it means to be loyal. You took me with you to every job, every position. Every start-up. You committed to me in a way that no one else in my life ever has.

And I don't know if you can possibly understand what that means for a foster kid who's had more houses than she can count."

Poppy stroked his face, her heart thundering hard, her whole body trembling. She continued, "You can't minimize the fact that you taught me that people can care that deeply. That they might show it in different ways, but that doesn't mean they don't care.

"I *do* know you have feelings, Isaiah. Because your actions show them. You are consistent month to month, year to year. It doesn't matter whether I misinterpret your reaction in the moment. You're always in it for the long haul. And that seems like a miracle to me." Her voice got thick, her eyes shiny. "You are not a trial, Isaiah Grayson. You are the greatest gift I've ever been given. And loving you is part of that gift."

The words washed over him, a balm for his soul. For his heart.

"I was afraid," he said. "Not just of being too much for you—" the words cut his throat "—but of losing you. I wish I were that altruistic. But I'm not. I was afraid because what I feel for you is so deep… I don't know what I would do if I lost you. If I… If I ruined it because of… Because of how I am."

"I *love* how you are." Poppy's voice was fierce. "It's up to me to tell you when something is wrong, to tell you when it's right. It doesn't matter how the rest of the world sees things, Isaiah. It matters how *we* see things. Here. Between us.

"Normal doesn't matter. Neither of us is normal. You're going to have to deal with my baggage. With the fact that I'm afraid I don't know how to be a mother because I never had one of my own. With the fact that sometimes my first instinct is to protect myself instead of fighting for what I feel. And I'm going to have to learn your way of communicating. That's love for everyone. Sometimes I'll be a bigger burden. And sometimes you will be. But we'll have each other. And that's so much better than being apart."

"I think I've loved you for a very long time. But it felt necessary to block it out. But once I touched you... Once I touched you, Poppy, I couldn't deny it. I can't keep you or my feelings for you in a box, and that terrifies me. You terrify me. But in a good way."

She lifted her hand, tracing a line down the side of his face. "The only thing that terrifies me is a life without you."

"Will you marry me? This time I'm asking. Not because you're pregnant. Not because I want a wife. Because I want you."

"I will marry you," she said. "Not for your family. Not in spite of you, but because of you. Because I love you."

"I might be bad when it comes to dealing with emotion, but I know right now I'm the happiest man in the world."

His heart felt like it might burst, and he didn't hide from it. Didn't push it aside. He opened himself up and embraced all of it.

"There will have to be some ground rules," Poppy said, smiling impishly.

"Ground rules?"

"Yes. Lines between our personal and professional lives. For example, at home, I'm not making the coffee."

"That's a sacrifice I'm willing to make."

"Good. But that won't be the only one."

He wrapped his arms around her and pulled them both into a standing position, Poppy cradled against his chest. "Why don't I take you into your bedroom and show you exactly what sorts of sacrifices I'm prepared to make."

"I don't have a bed in there," she protested as he carried her back toward her room. "There's just a sleeping bag."

"I think I can work with that."

And he did.

# Epilogue

December 24, 2018

WIFE FOUND—

Antisocial mountain man/businessman Isaiah Grayson married his assistant, his best friend and his other half, Poppy Sinclair, on Christmas Eve.

She'll give him a child or two, exact number to be negotiated. And has vowed to be as tolerant of his mood as he is of hers. Because that's how love works.

She is willing to stay with him in sickness and in health, in a mountain cabin or at a fancy

gala. As long as she is with him. For as long as
they both shall live.

She's happy for him to keep the beard.

They opted to have a small, family wedding on a
mountain.

The fact that Poppy was able to have a family
wedding made her heart feel like it was so full it
might burst. The Grayson clan was all in attendance,
standing in the snow, along with Rosalind and her
husband.

Poppy peeked out from around the tree she was
hiding behind and looked at Isaiah, who was standing next to Pastor John Thompson. The backdrop of
evergreens capped with snow was breathtaking, but
not as breathtaking as the man himself.

He wasn't wearing a suit. He was wearing a black
coat, white button-up shirt and black jeans. He also
had on his black cowboy hat. He hadn't shaved.

But that was what she wanted.

Him.

Not some polished version, but the man she loved.

This would be her new Christmas tradition. She
would think of her wedding. Of their love. Of how
her whole life had changed because of Isaiah Grayson.

For her part, Poppy had on her very perfect dress
and was holding a bouquet of dark red roses.

She smiled. It was the fantasy wedding she hadn't
even known she wanted.

But then, she supposed that was because she hadn't known who the groom might be.

But this was perfectly them. Remote, and yet surrounded by the people they loved most.

There was no music, just the deep silence of the forest, the sound of branches moving whenever there was a slight breeze. And Poppy came out from behind the tree when it felt like it was time.

She walked through the snow, her eyes never leaving Isaiah's. She felt like she might have been walking down a very long aisle toward him for the past ten years. And that each and every one of those years had been necessary to bring them to this moment.

Isaiah didn't feel things the way other people did. He felt them deeper. It took longer to get there, but she knew that now she had his heart, she would have it forever.

She trusted it. Wholly and completely.

Just like she trusted him.

He reached out and took her hand, and the two of them stood across from each other, love flooding Poppy's heart.

"I told you an ad was a good idea," he whispered after they'd taken their vows and the pastor had told him to kiss the bride.

"What are you talking about?"

"It's the reason I finally realized what was in front of me the whole time."

"I think we would have found our way without the ad."

"No. We needed the ad."

"So you can be right?" she asked, holding back a smile.

He grinned. "I'm always right."

"Oh, really? Well then, what do you think is going to happen next?"

He kissed her again, deep and hard and long. "I think we're going to live happily-ever-after."

He was right. As always.

* * * * *

# *CHAPTER ONE*

*New York City*

VASHTI ALCINDOR SHOULD be celebrating. After all, the official letter she'd just read declared her divorce final, which meant her three-year marriage to Scott Zimmons was over. Definitely done with. As far as she was concerned the marriage had lasted two years too long. She wouldn't count that first year since she'd been too in love to dwell on Scott's imperfections. Truth be told there were many that she'd deliberately overlooked. She'd been so determined to have that happily-ever-after that she honestly believed she could put up with anything.

But reality soon crept into the world of make-believe, and she discovered she truly couldn't. Her husband was a compulsive liar who could look you right in the eyes and lie with a straight face. She didn't want to count the number of times she'd caught him in the act. When she couldn't take the deceptions any longer she had packed her things and left. When her aunt Shelby died five months later, Scott felt entitled to half of the inheritance Vashti received in the will.

It was then that Vashti had hired one of the best divorce attorneys in New York, and within six weeks his private investigator had uncovered Scott's scandalous activities. Namely, his past and present affair with his boss's wife. Vashti hadn't wasted any time making Scott aware that she was not only privy to this information, but had photographs and videos to prove it.

Knowing she wouldn't hesitate to expose him as the lowlife that he was, Scott had agreed to an uncontested divorce and walked away with nothing. The letter she'd just read was documented proof that he would do just about anything to hold on to his cushy Wall Street job.

Her cell phone ringing snagged her attention, the ringtone belonging to her childhood friend and present Realtor, Bryce Witherspoon. Vashti clicked on her phone as she sat down at her kitchen table with her evening cup of tea. "Hey, girl, I hope you're calling with good news."

Bryce chuckled. "I am. Someone from the Barnes Group from California was here today and—"

"California?"

"Yes. They're a group of developers that's been trying to acquire land in the cove for years. They made you an unbelievably fantastic offer for Shelby by the Sea."

Vashti let out a loud shout of joy. She couldn't believe she'd been lucky enough to get rid of both her ex-husband and her aunt's property in the same day.

"Don't get excited yet. We might have problems," Bryce said.

Vashti frowned. "What kind of problems?"

"The developers want to tear down your aunt's bed-and-breakfast and—"

"Tear it down?" Vashti felt a soft kick in her stomach. Selling her aunt's bed-and-breakfast was one thing, having it demolished was another. "Why would they want to tear it down?"

"They aren't interested in the building, Vash. They want the eighty-five acres it sits on. Who wouldn't with the Gulf of Mexico in their backyard? I told you it would be a quick sale."

Vashti had known someone would find Shelby by the Sea a lucrative investment but she'd hoped somehow the inn would survive. With repairs it could be good as new. "What do they want to build there instead?"

"A luxury tennis resort."

Vashti nodded. "How much are they offering?" she asked, taking a sip of her tea.

"Ten million."

Vashti nearly choked. "Ten million dollars? That's nearly double what I was asking for."

"Yes, but the developers are eyeing the land next

to it, as well. I think they're hoping that one day Reid Lacroix will cave and sell his property. When he does, the developers will pounce on the opportunity to get their hands on it and build that golf resort they've been trying to put there for years. Getting your land will put their foot in the door so to speak."

Vashti took another sip of her tea. "What other problems are there?"

"This one is big. Mayor Proctor got wind of their offer and figured you might sell. He's calling a meeting."

"A meeting?"

"Yes, of the Catalina Cove zoning board. Although they can't stop you from selling the inn, they plan to block the buyer from bringing a tennis resort in here. The city ordinance calls for the zoning board to approve all new construction. This won't be the first time developers wanted to come into the cove and build something the city planners reject. Remember years ago when that developer wanted to buy land on the east end to build that huge shopping mall? The zoning board stopped it. They're determined that nothing in Catalina Cove changes."

"Well, it should change." As far as Vashti was concerned it was time for Mayor Proctor to get voted out. He had been mayor for over thirty years. When Vashti had left Catalina Cove for college fourteen years ago, developers had been trying to buy up the land for a number of progressive projects. The people of Catalina Cove were the least open-minded group she knew.

Vashti loved living in New York City where things were constantly changing and people embraced those changes. At eighteen she had arrived in the city to attend New York University and remained after getting a job with a major hotel chain. She had worked her way up to her six-figure salary as a hotel executive. At thirty-two she considered it her dream job. That wasn't bad for someone who started out working the concierge desk.

"Unless the Barnes Group can build whatever they want without any restrictions, there won't be a deal for us."

Vashti didn't like the sound of that. Ten million was ten million no matter how you looked at it. "Although I wouldn't want them to tear down Shelby, I think my aunt would understand my decision to do what's best for me." And the way Vashti saw it, ten million dollars was definitely what would be best for her.

"Do you really think she would want you to tear down the inn? She loved that place."

Vashti knew more than anyone how much Shelby by the Sea had meant to her aunt. It had become her life. "Aunt Shelby knew there was no way I would ever move back to Catalina Cove after what happened. Mom and Dad even moved away. There's no connection for me to Catalina Cove."

"Hey, wait a minute, Vash. I'm still here."

Vashti smiled, remembering how her childhood friend had stuck with her through thick and thin. "Yes, you're still there, which makes me think you need your head examined for not moving away when you could have."

"I love Catalina Cove. It's my home and need I remind you that for eighteen years it was yours, too."

"Don't remind me."

"Look, I know why you feel that way, Vash, but are you going to let that one incident make you have ill feelings about the town forever?"

"It was more than an incident, Bryce, and you know it." For Vashti, having a baby out of wedlock at sixteen had been a lot more than an incident. For her it had been a life changer. She had discovered who her real friends were during that time. Even now she would occasionally wonder how different things might have been had her child lived instead of died at birth.

"Sorry, bad choice of words," Bryce said, with regret in her voice.

"No worries. That was sixteen years ago." No need to tell Bryce that on occasion she allowed her mind to wander to that period of her life and often grieved for the child she'd lost. She had wanted children and Scott had promised they would start a family one day. That had been another lie.

"Tell me what I need to do to beat the rezoning board on this, Bryce," Vashti said, her mind made up.

"Unfortunately, to have any substantial input, you

need to meet with the board in person. I think it will be beneficial if the developers make an appearance, as well. According to their representative, they're willing to throw in a few perks that the cove might find advantageous."

"What kind of perks?"

"Free membership to the resort's clubhouse for the first year, as well as free tennis lessons for the kids for a limited time. It will also bring a new employer to town, which means new jobs. Maybe if they were to get support from the townsfolk, the board would be more willing to listen."

"What do you think are our chances?"

"To be honest, even with all that, it's a long shot. Reid Lacroix is on the board and he still detests change. He's still the wealthiest person in town, too, and has a lot of clout."

"Then why waste my and the potential buyer's time?"

"There's a slim chance time won't be wasted. K-Gee is on the zoning board and he always liked you in school. He's one of the few progressive members on the board and the youngest. Maybe he'll help sway the others."

Vashti smiled. Yes, K-Gee had liked her but he'd liked Bryce even more and they both knew it. His real name was Kaegan Chambray. He was part of the Pointe-au-Chien Native American tribe and his family's ties to the cove and surrounding bayou went back generations, before the first American settlers.

Although K-Gee was two years older than Vashti and Bryce, they'd hung together while growing up. When Vashti had returned to town after losing her baby, K-Gee would walk Vashti and Bryce home from school every day. Even though Bryce never said, Vashti suspected something happened between Bryce and K-Gee during the time Vashti was away at that unwed home in Arkansas.

"When did K-Gee move back to Catalina Cove, Bryce?"

"Almost two years ago to help out his mom and to take over his family's seafood supply business when his father died. His mother passed away last year. And before you ask why I didn't tell you, Vash, you know why. You never wanted to hear any news regarding what was happening in Catalina Cove."

No, she hadn't, but anything having to do with K-Gee wasn't just town news. Bryce should have known that. "I'm sorry to hear about his parents. I really am. I'm surprised he's on the zoning board."

For years the townsfolk of the cove had never recognized members of the Pointe-au-Chien Native American tribe who lived on the east side of the bayou. Except for when it was time to pay city taxes. With K-Gee on the zoning board that meant change was possible in Catalina Cove after all.

"I need to know what you want to do, Vash," Bryce said, interrupting her thoughts. "The Barnes Group is giving us twenty days to finalize the deal or they will withdraw their offer."

Vashti stood up to cross the kitchen floor and put her teacup in the kitchen sink. "Okay, I'll think about what you said. Ten million dollars is a lot of money."

"Yes, and just think what you could do with it."

Vashti was thinking and she loved all the possibilities. Although she loved her job, she could stop working and spend the rest of her life traveling to all those places her aunt always wanted to visit but hadn't, because of putting Shelby by the Sea first. Vashti wouldn't make the same mistake.

THE NEXT MORNING, for the first time in two years, Vashti woke up feeling like she was in control of her life and could finally see a light—a bright one at that—at the end of the road. Scott was out of her life, she had a great job, but more importantly, some developer group was interested in her inn.

*Her inn.*

It seemed odd to think of Shelby by the Sea as hers when it had belonged to her aunt for as long as she could remember. Definitely long before Vashti was born. Her parents' home had been a mile away, and growing up she had spent a lot of her time at Shelby; especially during her teen years when she worked as her aunt's personal assistant. That was when she'd fallen in love with the inn and had thought it was the best place in the world.

Until…

Vashti pushed the "until" from her mind, refusing to go there and hoping Bryce was wrong about her having to return to Catalina Cove to face off with the rezoning board. There had to be another way and she intended to find it. Barely eighteen, she had needed to escape the town that had always been her safe haven because it had become a living hell for her.

An hour later Vashti had showered, dressed and was walking out her door ready to start her day at the Grand Nunes Luxury Hotel in Manhattan. But not before stopping at her favorite café on the corner to grab a blueberry muffin and a cup of coffee. Catalina Cove was considered the blueberry capital in the country, and even she couldn't resist this small indulgence from her hometown. She would be the first to admit that although this blueberry muffin was delicious, it was not as good as the ones Bryce's mother made and sold at their family's restaurant.

With the bag containing her muffin in one hand and her cup of coffee in the other, Vashti caught the elevator up to the hotel's executive floor. She couldn't wait to get to work.

She'd heard that the big man himself, Gideon Nunes, was in town and would be meeting with several top members of the managerial and executive team, which would include her.

It was a half hour before lunch when she received a call to come to Mr. Nunes's office. Ten minutes later she walked out of the CEO's office stunned, in a state of shock. According to Mr. Nunes, his five hotels in the States had been sold, including this one. He'd further stated that the new owner was bringing in his own people, which meant her services were no longer needed.

In other words, she'd been fired.

# CHAPTER TWO

*A week later*

VASHTI GLANCED AROUND the Louis Armstrong New Orleans International Airport. Although she'd never returned to Catalina Cove, she'd flown into this airport many times to attend a hotel conference or convention, or just to get away. Even though Catalina Cove was only an hour's drive away, she'd never been tempted to take the road trip to revisit the parish where she'd been born.

Today, with no job and more time on her hands than she really needed or wanted, in addition to the fact that there was ten million dollars dangling in front of her face, she was returning to Catalina Cove to attend the zoning board meeting and plead her case, although the thought of doing so was a bitter pill to swallow. When she'd left the cove she'd felt she didn't owe the town or its judgmental people anything. Likewise, they didn't owe her a thing. Now fourteen years later she was back and, to her way of thinking, Catalina Cove did owe her something.

# Get 4 FREE REWARDS!

## We'll send you 2 FREE Books plus 2 FREE Mystery Gifts.

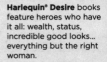

**Harlequin® Desire** books feature heroes who have it all: wealth, status, incredible good looks... everything but the right woman.

FREE Value Over $20

His eyes dipped briefly to her lips, igniting a sizzle in the air that had no place being there after he'd shared the sad story of his past. Even so, her answering reaction was to study his firm mouth in contemplation. The barely there scruff lining his angled jaw. His dominating presence made her feel fragile yet safe at the same time.

The urge to comfort him—to comfort herself—lingered. This time she didn't deny it.

With her free hand she reached up and cupped the thick column of his neck, tugging him down. He resisted, but only barely, stopping short a brief distance from her mouth to mutter one word.

"Hey..."

She didn't know if he'd meant to follow it with "this is a bad idea" or "we shouldn't get carried away," but she didn't wait to find out.

Her lips touched his gently and his mouth answered by puckering to return the kiss. Her eyes sank closed and his hand flinched against her palm.

He tasted…amazing. Like spiced cider and a capable, strong, heartbroken man who kept his hurts hidden from the outside world.

Eyes closed, she gripped the back of his neck tighter, angling her head to get more of his mouth. And when he pulled his hand from hers to come to rest on her shoulder, she swore she might melt from lust from that casual touch. His tongue came out to play, tangling with hers in a sensual, forbidden dance.

She used that free hand to fist his undershirt, tugging it up and brushing against the plane of his firm abs, and Emmett's response was to lift the hem of her sweater, where his rough fingertips touched the exposed skin of her torso.

A tight, needy sound escaped her throat, and his lips abruptly stopped moving against hers.

He pulled back, blinking at her with lust-heavy lids. She touched her mouth and looked away, the heady spell broken.

She'd just kissed her brother's best friend—a man who until today she might have jokingly described as her mortal enemy.

Worse, Emmett had kissed her back.

It was okay for this to be pretend—for their wedding to be an arrangement—but there was nothing black-and-white between them any longer. There was real attraction—as volatile as a live wire and as dangerous as a downed electric pole.

Whatever line they'd drawn by agreeing to marry, she'd stepped way, way over it.

He sobered quickly, recovering faster than she did. When he spoke, he echoed the words in her mind.

"That was a mistake."

*Don't miss what happens next!*
*A Christmas Proposition by Jessica Lemmon,*
*part of her Dallas Billionaires Club series!*

*Available December 2018 wherever*
*Harlequin® Desire books and ebooks are sold.*

www.Harlequin.com

Want to give in to temptation with
steamy tales of irresistible desire?

Check out **Harlequin® Presents®,
Harlequin® Desire** and
**Harlequin® Kimani™ Romance** books!

**New books available every month!**

**CONNECT WITH US AT:**

Facebook.com/groups/HarlequinConnection

 Facebook.com/HarlequinBooks

 Twitter.com/HarlequinBooks

 Instagram.com/HarlequinBooks

Pinterest.com/HarlequinBooks

ReaderService.com

**ROMANCE WHEN
YOU NEED IT**

PGENRE2018

# *Love Harlequin romance?*

## DISCOVER.

Be the first to find out about promotions,
news and exclusive content!

 Facebook.com/HarlequinBooks

Twitter.com/HarlequinBooks

 Instagram.com/HarlequinBooks

 Pinterest.com/HarlequinBooks

ReaderService.com

## EXPLORE.

Sign up for the Harlequin e-newsletter and
download a free book from any series at
**TryHarlequin.com.**

## CONNECT.

Join our Harlequin community to share
your thoughts and connect with other
romance readers!
**Facebook.com/groups/HarlequinConnection**

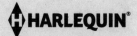

**ROMANCE WHEN
YOU NEED IT**